Del

DEFYING MAGICK

Debbie Cassidy

This book is a work of fiction. Names, characters, businesses, organizations, places, events, and incidents either are the product of the author's imagination or are used fictitiously. Any resemblance to actual persons, living or dead, events, or locales is entirely coincidental

Cover by Covers by Julie

1

"Damn, Honey. Why didn't you tell us your friend was so hawt?" Finley, Honey's brother, said.

"Shut it, Finley," Kieran, their older sibling, shoved him aside. He turned to me and gave me a mock bow. "Forgive my impudent brother, my lady. Would you consider taking a stroll with me through the moonlit forest?" He grinned cheekily. "I promise I won't bite unless you ask me to."

"Shut it, both of you." Honey waved them away.

They backed up, nudging each other. "Oh, come on, Hon. You gotta learn to share," Finley said. "Carmella, you want to have some fun?"

It *was* tempting. The identical twins were yum. Kieran was older by five minutes and slightly more buff than his sibling. Another time, another place, and who knows—but the party girl, the one used to getting her heart trampled on, was gone.

"Tempting, but I'll pass." I smiled to soften the rejection.

"Aw, you have no idea what you're missing." Finley winked.

"Hey, Fin!" a female voice called out.

He glanced over his shoulder at the petite brunette hailing him and then turned to us with a naughty smile. "Looks like I just got me a booty call."

Kieran sighed, his gaze hooded. "Just be careful."

Finley slapped him on the back. "Always." He sauntered off toward the woman.

"Why didn't you tell him?" Honey asked Kieran, hands on hips.

Kieran shrugged and scuffed the ground with the toe of his boot. "He wouldn't have believed me. Best he finds out for himself." He gave me a soft smile. "See you later, Carmella."

I turned to Honey. "What was that about?"

Her lip curled. “The slag, Roni, that’s what. She strung Kieran along for a month and then dumped him, and now she’s gunning for Finley, even though she knows they’re brothers. I don’t know what she’s trying to prove.”

“Aside from the fact that she has no class?”

Honey chuckled.

These were Honey’s people, her family, and they’d adopted me so easily even though I wasn’t yaksha. It was unusual for an outsider to be allowed to a Yaksha gathering. But Honey had drafted me into helping with the catering, so here we were. Yeah, I hadn’t been too keen on the whole idea at first. Being stuck in the forest with a bunch of yaksha didn’t really sound too appealing, but Honey was a friend. I trusted her not to eat me or let me be eaten, and so far, all the yaksha had been chowing down on was the food we’d brought.

The gatherings happened once or twice a year. Key members of all the packs got together to discuss territory and politics, and when they were done, they ran, ate, fucked, and howled at the moon. Here on the outskirts of London, surrounded by forest and greenery and the scent of moist earth, it was easy to forget the manic hustle of the inner city. The stars were bright here—tiny gems nestling in a blanket of darkness—with the moon, a silver-white disc, taking center stage.

"Honey." Gareth, Honey's father, joined us. "Why don't you take your friend for a walk?"

It wasn't really a request.

Honey made an O with her mouth and then grabbed my hand. "Come on. Let me show you my special spot."

We wound our way through the tents and campfires. Yaksha raised their heads to either watch us pass or to hail Honey. She seemed popular.

We broke out of the barrier of brightly lit lamps planted in the ground and headed up a grassy knoll.

Honey dropped to the ground at the top, legs out in front of her. "Sit." She patted the spot next to her.

I parked my butt and tilted my head up to the sky. "Wow. That is one huge moon."

Honey sighed. "It's always so peaceful here."

"Hey, Vanessa. Come suck on my cock!" someone shouted. Several howls followed.

I turned to her. "You were saying?"

She nudged me with her shoulder. "You know what I mean."

Yeah, I so did. This was a nature enthusiast's paradise. Far from the city buzz, except I kinda liked the buzz. It was a soothing lullaby. Out here, in the fresh air and relative silence, the world felt like a larger place, open and raw and dangerous. A shiver ran up my spine. Banner was right. You could invite a city girl to the country, but you couldn't make her want to stay. If there'd been an option of heading back, I'd have jumped at it. But Honey was my friend, and this was important to her, so I fixed my gaze on the clearing below which was ringed by lamps. At least fifty tents dotted the green, accompanied by several small campfires.

Strange to see so many beasts acting so human.

"I know what you're thinking," Honey said.

"Oh, really?"

"Yeah, you're wondering how we can be so civilized."

"Well, the thought had crossed my mind."

She chuckled. “We’re not so different from you, you know.”

“Aside from the fangs and the hair?”

She shrugged. “We’re both animals. It’s just our instincts to hunt are stronger. And yes, there’s the fangs and the hair too.” She picked at her shirt. “I used to fucking hate it. I used to wish I could just be normal, you know? Even convinced my mum to send me to a regular school. No one knew what I was for two years. I had human friends, and then there was an incident. I got invited to a party, and the girl had a dog. Well … you can imagine what happened.”

Yep, I sure could. “The dog went berserk when he smelled you.”

She snorted. “It attacked me. The fucking thing was huge, twice the size of an eight-year-old, and I was a pretty small eight-year-old. So, I defended myself the only way I knew how.”

“Oh, shit.”

“Yeah.”

We fell into silence, watching the commotion below—the good-natured yells and the camaraderie between packs.

Pulling my legs up, I wrapped my arms around them. “Why can’t it always be like this?”

Honey leaned back on her elbows. “Because we’re constantly walking the line between higher intelligence and primitive instinct. The higher intelligence part tells us to communicate in words, to set up treaties and build alliances, while all the primitive side wants to do is piss all over its territory and kill anyone who intrudes.”

“I love your way with words.”

She flicked her ponytail. “Yeah, it’s a gift. Speaking of gifts, when are you getting yours cut off?”

I groaned and rested my forehead on my knees. “Don’t ask. It was supposed to be two days ago, but the High Witch hit a glitch with the spell so she postponed till Sunday.”

“So, two days left?”

“Yeah.” Two days left till my witch blood status was taken away.

Down below us, the yaksha gathered into a close knit group. “What’s going on?”

Honey licked her lips and delved into her bag. "The best bit." She pulled out a pair of binoculars. "Shit is gonna get naked."

Naked? Oh, my God. Were they taking off their clothes? Was that why her dad had asked her to bring me up here?

"Let me see." I yanked the binoculars off her and peered down into the lamp-lit clearing. Bare muscled torsos and thick powerful thighs and … Wow. These guys were hung.

Honey snorted. "I fucking love this bit."

Then they began to morph and shift, their bodies rippling and contorting. My stomach flipped, not in disgust, but in wonder. They were magnificent primal beings; scary as heck but still amazing.

Honey tried to pry the binoculars from my hand just as shadowy movement in the tree line caught my eye.

"Wait." I jerked away from her, focusing on the spot where I'd caught the motion.

"Oh, like that, is it?"

"There's something out there."

"What?"

“I saw something in the tree line.” There was no movement now. “Probably an animal?”

Honey snorted. “No animal will be coming anywhere near this clearing for a good few days, not with the scent of all these predators in the air.”

Shit, she had a point. Maybe I’d imagined it? No. There is was again.

“Carmella? What is it?” Her tone was tense.

The Yaksha were howling at the moon now, all shifted into their half beast, half man forms.

“I don’t know, I thought I—”

Several male figures exploded into the clearing. They were surrounded by shifting shadows and each carried silver blades and … whips? Shit, what the fuck?

Honey let out a squeal, and the binoculars slipped from my fingers. Below us, the clearing erupted in growls and roars as the Yaksha met the attack head on. The attackers were sorely outnumbered. At least seventy Yaksha to thirteen shadow-coated men, but the intruders seemed unfazed, swinging their blades and cracking their whips. Honey was on her feet, her body vibrating with the need for action.

But it was okay. Whoever these men were, they'd be no match for the Yaksha. Then one of the dudes with a whip lassoed a yaksha by the neck and tugged, and the yaksha's head came clean off. The whip glowed neon blue before settling back into silver again.

Honey screamed and dropped to the ground, her body shifting so fast my eyes couldn't keep up.

"Stay here," she growled, and then she was no longer the woman I knew.

She was full beast—all humanity gone. She was something else, something rare. Only a handful of yaksha could go full beast, and she was the first one I'd met. She turned her massive, muzzled head my way, and if not for the glint of humanity in her eyes, I'd have lost bladder control. She bounded down the rise into the fray.

My heart slammed against my ribcage in delayed fear-mode.

The clearing was chaos: dead yaksha, glowing silver blades, whips, snarls, growls, and roars. Honey cut a swath through the carnage, bee-lining for the back of the fray, where her father and brothers had pitched our tents.

Who were these creatures? Why were they attacking the packs? Darkness writhed around them, making it difficult to make out their facial features. These weren't the same monsters who had attacked and almost killed me. These were something new. Through the binoculars, I caught a flash of fur, bone, and the twin glow of eyes. Honey was standing over a body. Impossible to make out whose, but she was protecting it, so it was either one of her brothers or her dad. Shit, the guy with the whip was moving toward her, probably downwind of her. She wasn't going to see him or smell him in time. I was on the move before I'd had time to think it through, bounding down the rise and into the clearing, dodging and ducking my way toward my friend.

"Honey! Honey, watch out!"

Her ears pricked up, and she tensed, locking gazes with me. I was close, but he was closer.

The whip whizzed through the air. Honey turned her head and something inside me shifted. One moment, I was three meters away, and the next, I was between the whip and Honey.

His eyes flashed and widened. The whip hissed as it cut through the air.

It was going to hit me.

2

The tail of the whip hurtled toward me. Honey roared and shoved my butt with her bulk, trying to knock me off balance and push me out of the way. My body was immovable, the power that had allowed me to speed-move held me rooted to the spot now. A part of me screamed to dive out of the way, to save myself, but the kernel of power inside me pulsed and raged at me to stand firm. There was no way he was getting to her. I brought up my hand to shield my face, and the whip slapped against it, winding around my palm. The contact was searing hot, and the scent of burning flesh filled the air. My burning flesh! Oh, shit! The pain hit a moment later, setting my nerve endings on fire. A scream tore from my throat just as the kernel associated with my asura power opened, and an answering flare of power shot up my arm and attacked the whip. It glowed red, then slid from my flesh with a hiss.

Honey bolted around me and launched herself at the guy. The shadows surrounded her, tearing at her.

"Honey!"

Darkness swallowed me as I threw myself at the attacker, and then we were being shoved back by an invisible force. Butt meet ground, and was that a flying yaksha? Honey hit the grass to my left but was back on her feet in an instant, barreling toward the figure. The man backed up, his dark eyes were narrow slits fixed on me.

"Not just yet." His lips curled in a mercenary smile. And then the shadow turned to mist, obscuring him completely. Honey shot straight through the vapor.

The man was gone.

Around us, the howls and growls died down, and the clearing fell into an ominous silence. The wind rustled through the trees surrounding us, taunting us with the normality of nature.

Oh, God. Fucking God. Bodies—cut, torn, and lifeless—lay across a forest floor wet with blood. Pulling myself up, I took a step toward the carnage. A space that a moment ago had been filled with life, was now shrouded in death. Numbness warred with the heat of anger. Anger won, infusing my limbs with renewed strength.

"Carmella … What?" Honey's voice was a desperate rasp. She was back in human form.

All the yaksha were dead. Seventy powerful beasts cut down by thirteen assailants. No saving them, no helping them, but Honey, I could help Honey. My knees hit the dirt beside her trembling form.

Gareth, her father, stared unblinking at the sky. His mouth was parted as if in surprise at finding his guts lying on the grass beside him.

"Gone … they're all gone." She raised her head and locked gazes with me. Her lips trembled, and she covered her mouth, her dark eyes huge above her hand.

It was the urge to scream and release the shock, pain and horror. It bubbled up in my throat too, but I swallowed it, reaching for my phone in my back pocket instead. Honey didn't question who I was calling. Too focused on controlling erratic breaths as she struggled to keep it together.

The adrenaline was ebbing, and gripping the phone with white-knuckled hands to stem the tremor, I hit speed dial. Melody Parker, head of the Alpha patrol for the IEPEU answered on the fourth ring.

"Hunter? What's wrong? Need a pick up from the hairy gathering?"

I swallowed the lump in my throat. "Parker, I'm going to need a forensics unit and … morgue vans."

Parker was silent for a long beat. "How many vans?"

"Enough for seventy Yaksha."

"Hold tight. We're on our way."

No questions, no probing, just action. Parker was on her way. Dropping the phone, I reached for Honey and pulled her into my arms, rocking her back and forth, not sure if it was to comfort her or me. Several long minutes ticked by.

Honey eased out the embrace. "I'm going to find the bastards that did this." Her tone was ice shards.

"I'm going to find them, and I'm going to tear their goddamn hearts out."

The ice that had filled my veins melted into a simmering heat. "We'll find them. We'll find the bastards together."

THE PLACE WAS crawling with suited and armed IEPEU agents. Choppers *whumped* above us—their search-lights scanning the area for our assailants. They wouldn't find anything. The killers were long gone.

Melody made notes on the descriptions Honey and I had given her. She pocketed her notepad and pen and turned her attention to Honey. "I'm sorry about for your loss, Miss Dante."

"I need to contact the families of the … the dead," Honey said. "I need to make a list."

Melody's lips thinned. "No. You need to go home and let us deal with this. We can contact the relevant parties."

Honey pulled herself up to her full five-foot-seven height. “These are my people, and I’m not leaving until every last one has been identified and bagged.”

Melody nodded. “Fine. In that case, we better get to work.”

I didn’t know any of the yaksha here aside from Honey’s family, but there was no way I was leaving her to do this alone. It took hours. Some bodies were so badly maimed Honey couldn’t figure out who they were, and by the end, it became a process of elimination. But after two hours, we’d identified them all. Honey’s brothers and father were the last to be loaded into the morgue van, and throughout it all, Honey didn’t shed a single tear. The final van drove out of the clearing, and the IEPEU began to pack up.

Melody joined us. “We’re done here for now. A team will sweep the area again once it’s light. You want a lift home?”

“Home …” Honey blinked slowly.

Shit. Her dad and brothers were her only family. And most of her pack was dead, what would she be going home to?

I put an arm around Honey's shoulder and addressed Melody. "Can you drop us at my place?"

Melody nodded curtly. "Sure."

The drive back was mostly silent. Honey fell asleep in the back—a blessing to shut out the horrific reality of what had just happened.

I kept my eyes on the road. "I want in on this case."

Melody sighed. "I thought you might. Thing is, aside from the fact that you've only been with us for a week, it's not advisable to work a case you're so close to."

"I know."

She glanced at Honey in the rearview mirror. "I'll pull some strings. Do my best to get you on it. Just, try to keep your friend out of it. I know it'll be difficult, but she's going to have a load of shit to deal with now. A mass murder investigation is the last thing she needs."

"What do you mean?"

Melody's lips tightened. "How much do you know about Yaksha inter-pack politics?"

"Not much. Just that a bunch of representatives and their families meet a couple of times a year to connect and hash stuff out."

"Yeah, that's the civilized aspect of the whole thing. But there's been a power play between the packs for decades. The Renegade Pack is the most business orientated pack out of the six active packs we know of. Their eateries bring in a ton of revenue, and a couple of other packs, Moonlight and Shakti, have been trying to buy them out for years. Gareth Dante had been resistant to offers of investment and partnership. That business meant the world to him. With him gone, the new heads of the pack are gonna come gunning for Honey. A female in charge of an empire … the alpha males aren't gonna stand for that. The treaties agreed by the old alphas died with those yaksha. A new order is on the horizon. Your friend is going to need her focus to navigate the stormy waters ahead."

"Yeah, well, she won't have to do it alone."

Melody smiled. "I didn't think so." We pulled into the lot behind the Delightful Bakery. "How are things with Banner?"

"I haven't spoken to him in a few days. He *likes* me."

"Yeah, I figured that might be the case. He has this look in his eyes when he speaks about you."

"He does?"

She nodded. "Oh, before I forget. Update. After you told me about the Ghandarva feather and how Banner, Vritra, and Shukra were the only others that knew about it, I requested a surveillance on the three guys."

"And?"

"Well, they wouldn't approve it for Banner. As much as I hate to admit it, the covens have way too much influence on the IEPEU activities, and surveillance on their witches, especially an elder witch, is a huge no-no. But we have been keeping tabs on Vritra and Shukra best we can, considering the high security of that place, but so far nothing to suggest anything nefarious."

"Maybe the information got out some other way? Like I said at the time, Banner was gathering items for the spell. Someone could have cottoned on."

Her mouth twisted in thought. “It’s looking more and more likely, which sucks because it means we’re totally in the dark again.” She sighed. “I’ll see you at work tomorrow.”

“You’ll get me on the case?”

“I’ll do my best.”

Honey stirred in the back. Her eyes opened, and for a moment her expression was clear and untroubled, and then her face pinched in pain and her lips quivered. She pressed them together and turned to look out the passenger side window.

“We here?” she asked.

“Yeah.”

“Thank you.” She nodded in Melody’s direction and then climbed out of the car.

“Let me know if you need anything,” Melody said softly. “If she needs anything.”

“I will.” I joined Honey by the metal steps leading up to my flat.

We watched Melody drive off before climbing the steps. I unlocked the door and entered, but Honey remained in the doorway looking dazed.

“Honey?”

She blew out a breath. "Did it really happen?"

Oh, God. I wish I could say no. That it was all a bad dream. "Yeah. It did."

She walked over to the sofa and sat down. "It was a hit."

"What?"

She looked up, her expression hard. "It had to be a hit—all the most influential yaksha in one place at the same time—someone ordered a hit. I don't know who the killers were, but that doesn't matter, not really. We need to find out who ordered the hit."

"It makes sense, but who'd want all the alphas dead?"

She snorted. "Any number of ambitious betas. Heck, maybe they banded together and organized the hit so they could take power over the packs."

"There weren't any betas at the gathering?"

She swallowed hard. "There was one. Kieran. General rule is that you either get one or the other at any political event. Gatherings are alpha domain. Their close family members also attend. Father asked Kieran to stay behind, but he insisted on coming." She dropped her head into her hands. "Oh, fuck.

Renegade has no beta. Whoever organized this took out the heads of every pack, leaving the hierarchy open to new rule. Everything we've worked toward, all the boundaries we've set up will be in question. And my pack … we're fucked."

Yeah, this theory was sounding more and more likely by the second. A beta would have motive. But I had to ask, "Is there anyone else aside from the betas who may have a grudge against the Yaksha? Did the packs have issues with anyone else?"

She snorted derisively. "We're too busy having issues amongst ourselves to worry about anyone else. The Yaksha community is pretty egocentric."

"Okay, so we figure out who these guys that attacked us are, and we get them to lead us back to whoever ordered the hit."

"I've never seen anything like them."

"Me either. But they were definitely supernatural, and if the IEPEU have tangled with them before, the system will pull up the details."

"And if not?"

"Then we go to the gods." If the IEPEU didn't have a record, then the only other beings that may know what these creatures are would be the gods. They had been here for the birth of all the supernatural races after all.

She sat up straighter. “You could get access to the gods at Brahma Corp through the IEPEU, right?”

No need to tell her that I didn’t need the IEPEU to get access to the gods. I’d met Indra and Varuna five years ago when the world had almost gone to shit. They’d help me if I asked, no doubt.

“Yeah. Melody will do her best to get me on this case, but even if she can’t, I *will* find out what happened to your family. I promise you, you’ll have justice.”

Honey’s jaw tensed. “I know you will. But I’m not going to sit back and twiddle my thumbs while you do it.”

Melody was right, keeping Honey out of the investigation was the wise move, but wise wasn’t always the right move. Her family had been taken from her, murdered right before her eyes. Shutting her out was not an option.

“I don’t expect you to, but first you need to take care of business. Your pack business.”

Her breath whooshed out. “Oh, fuck. The eateries.”

“Yeah.”

She pinched the bridge of her nose. “I need to get home.”

“Yeah. First thing tomorrow. Get some sleep and then—”

“No.” She was on her feet. “The vultures will be circling looking for weakness. If they find out I ran and hid I’ll be discredited, deemed unfit to run the empire my father created.” She walked over to the door. “The betas are probably meeting now. I need to be there to represent Renegade.”

“But, you’re not a beta.”

She gave me a tired smile. “No. With dad and Kieran gone, I’m the new alpha.”

3

My sleep had been fitful, filled with nightmares of shadows and death, and I was glad to get to the office in the morning. The building was situated on the South Bank, and my desk was on the third floor by the windows, with an awesome view of the river. But even the serene body of water did nothing to sooth me today.

Honey was an alpha. Apparently alphas and betas weren't voted in, they were born—some kind of genetic thing—and Honey had the alpha gene. There were always one or two yaksha with the gene in any pack, but the most dominant one became Alpha, and the second most dominant took the beta role, moving up only when the alpha stepped down or died.

Operatives trickled in behind me. It didn't matter that it was a Saturday. The IEPEU worked any and all hours, although numbers were considerably lighter on the weekends. The floor was an open plan with each desk having its own corkboard and white board. The majority of which were covered in marker pen and photographs. Mine was embarrassingly bare, but that was to be expected with only a week on the job, most of which had been orientation and training. If Melody swung it, this would be my first case—a huge case. Come to think of it, it was highly unlikely that Parker would succeed in convincing them to let me run point on this a week into the job.

"Hey, Hunter." Mason raised his coffee cup in greeting as he passed.

The older guy was close to retirement age and spent most of his time telling stories about his favorite cases, and very little time actually doing any work. But it was obvious from the way the rest of the staff spoke about him, that the place wouldn't be the same without him.

My phone rang, and Vritra flashed on caller ID. I just didn't have the energy for his concern right now.

It'd be the same mantra. Come live at Shaitan Enterprises, be with the asura, embrace the asura, lick the damn asura … Hmmm, he'd probably like that. A shiver ran through me, because maybe I'd like it too. No. Go away dirty thoughts. But seriously the man's middle name was *persistence,* and it was working, he was wearing me down. My witch status was being taken away tomorrow, and all I'd have left was my asura side. Common sense dictated the importance of finding out about my asura heritage. Curiosity asserting that I find out who the fuck my father was. But there were two cases to solve first. Karen, the crazy Daayan who wanted to kill me, and the Yaksha massacre. No option but to hit ignore on his call.

My gaze snagged on the dark haired, stubble-faced figure of the most experienced investigative officer in the office. Murdoch glanced up as if sensing my regard, and his green eyes focused on me through his Clark Kent spectacles. I raised a hand in greeting, and he inclined his head in acknowledgment. The guy was a legend in this place, with almost one hundred cases under his belt, all solved. There wasn't a cold case to his name. In fact, he was actually working his way through the cold cases on file. Yeah, the man was a genius and kind of intimidating.

Dumping my bag at my desk, I picked up my phone and dialed Melody's office.

She answered almost immediately. "Check your emails."

"I got the case?"

"Sort of."

"Sort of?"

She sighed. "Look, you're a newbie with no proven track record, aside from uncovering the lab, which I made sure to point out. But this is a high-profile case, and the heads of allocations were totally against it, so I offered a compromise."

My stomach sank. "What kind of compromise?"

"You get to run point on the case, but you report to a senior officer."

There were only two senior officers I could think of who allocations may have picked. Please say Mason, please say Mason. "Who?"

"Murdoch."

Oh, fuck.

"Hunter?"

"I'm here. Okay. I can do that."

"You report to Murdoch, and Murdoch will keep the team informed. Remember, no rushing into active scenes. Your duty extends to investigative only."

"I get it."

"The team is sweeping the area again this morning, and they'll pass any new information to you. And Hunter?"

"Yeah?"

"Good luck."

I dropped the phone back into its cradle just as a shadow fell over me.

"Hunter." Murdoch said, towering over me from his six-foot-something height. "I assume that was Parker."

I nodded. "Excited to be working with you."

"*For* me. You'll be working *for* me."

For him? My hackles rose. Hell, no. "Last I checked I worked for the IEPEU. I *report* to you, but this is *my* case."

He stared at me levelly for a long beat, probably expecting me to be intimidated and back down. Ignoring the anxiety in my belly, I glared right back.

"Okay then." He perched on the edge of my desk.

Huh? What had just happened?

"So tell me, what's your first move?" he asked, all casual-like.

"I need to identify the creatures that attacked the gathering."

"Yes, the description was put into the system. No hits I'm afraid, so what now?"

Was this some kind of test? "I didn't think there would be. I've never seen anything like them, but I know who may have."

He arched a brow.

"The gods."

He nodded. "Good plan. You'll need a Warrant for Information form, number E54. I'll sign it for you."

"Um, I think I'll be fine without it."

"Really? And how do you intend to obtain a meeting with the gods? Just walk in and ask to speak to them at reception?"

"Well, yeah, actually."

He stared at me blankly.

"I kinda know them."

“You know the gods?”

“Yeah.”

His eyes narrowed. “Well, maybe there is a reason they handed this case to a total noob.” His tone was more speculative than insulting. “Report back what you find. I’ll be here.”

Yeah, he was always here. The other operatives joked that the guy practically lived at the office. This job was his life. There was a story there, but no one seemed to know it—a helluva lot of speculation and not enough facts. It didn’t speak well for the investigative operatives’ skills, but whatever.

My mobile buzzed, and Honey’s name flashed on caller ID.

“Hey, Honey. How’d it go with the betas?”

“It didn’t, not yet. The meeting is scheduled for tonight. Did you get the case?”

“Yes. I have to report to another operative, but I’m taking lead. I’m just about to head to Brahma Corp to see Indra.”

“I’ll meet you there.”

No reason why she couldn't tag along. I'd promised not to shut her out so … "See you in forty minutes."

Hanging up and grabbing my bag, I headed for the lifts. My phone buzzed again, Urvashi this time.

"Carmella! Thank God you're okay. I heard what happened at the gathering."

"I'm fine. Just on the case now."

"The same case? Oh, babe. Do you think you should?"

"I have to." I pressed the call button on the lift.

"Any news on Karen?"

The High Witch had been clear that we were on a deadline with finding Karen, but it had been a week and the Daayan hadn't come for me. The pearl the High Witch had given me was tucked in the side pocket of my bag. It went everywhere with me, just in case.

"What if she doesn't come for you?" Urvashi asked. "What if she just hides?"

It was a possibility the High Witch hadn't considered. How much time did we have? Maybe it was time to become the hunter.

"I'm seeing the High Witch on Saturday, so I'll ask her then. There has to be some way to track Karen down. If the covens put their heads together, maybe we can trace her and end this."

The lift arrived. "I've got to dash, but pop over this evening if you like."

"I'll bring dinner."

"Even better."

My cuff caught the light as I stepped into the lift. What was Paimon doing right now? Nope, don't think about it. He'd promised to tell me when Alara regained consciousness. But a week had gone by with no contact. Surely, she was awake by now. Maybe they were making up for lost time in his wonder bed. Urgh!

Dammit, stop thinking about him.

My cuff had been on when the yaksha were attacked, but I hadn't thought to call to him. I'd simply reacted. By somehow tapping into my asura power, I'd survived.

Ha, maybe I didn't need his protection after all. A hollow feeling bloomed in my chest. Not needing him every single time didn't mean I'd never need him, right? The cuff could stay. There was still Karen to consider. She could catch me unawares. Yeah. The cuff was useful. Okay, so the darn thing was turning into a comfort blanket—familiar and safe when too many things in my life were chopping and changing. Tomorrow my connection to the skein would be cut off, and I'd no longer be a witch.

Another change.

The cuff was my constant … for now.

The lift spat me out in the front foyer and my phone buzzed again. It sucked that I needed to almost die for people to call me, but then I checked the caller ID and my heart skipped a beat.

It was Aaron, one of my closest friends, and someone I hadn't heard from in weeks. He'd been drafted by the IEPEU when the guild had shut down, and then transferred to another department out of town. Man, I missed him, but damn, I was annoyed with him. No contact, not a single fucking call since he'd left. Like, what was up with that? I stepped out into the warm breeze and answered.

"Hello, stranger." My tone was icy.

"Carm, thank God you're okay. I just got back from a mission, and I heard about the lab. I heard what happened. I'm so sorry I wasn't there."

As much as I'd like to be magnanimous about his absence, I couldn't. I was pissed. We were buddies, or at least we had been before his transfer. "Where were you? I called you like, loads and your phone went to voicemail."

"I can't tell you that. It's classified."

Yeah, well my friendship was classified. Gah! Damn the IEPEU. How could I blame him for doing his job? "I'm fine. But I have to go."

"You're mad. I get it."

My eyes pricked. Fuck being mad. "I miss you."

"Oh, babe. I miss you too. Look. I have a few days off, and I'm gonna swing by and see you, 'kay? We can do our movie night, grab Malina and Garuda and …"

"They're in Nagalok."

"What? Since when?"

"About a month now. You know how time runs differently between our worlds."

"Don't I just. Wait, you were alone when this happened?"

My throat began to close up. Do not feel sorry for yourself, dammit. "Not exactly, but I'll explain when you come see me."

"I'll be there midweek. Love you, babe."

"Love you too."

The aerial tram station loomed up ahead, across the main road. I made to step out just as a limo slid to a halt right in front of me.

The back passenger door opened, and Vritra leaned out. "Get in."

His ember eyes were blazing with suppressed fury.

Oh, dear.

4

Vritra glared at me from the seat opposite me. "Good to see you alive and well, Miss Hunter."

Why had I got into the car again? "Look. You have to stop doing this—calling, checking up on me. I'm not your responsibility, okay?"

He let out a bark of laughter. "If only that were true."

What the heck was that supposed to mean? "I have a case, and I need to be somewhere, so if we're done here …" I reached for the door handle, and he leaned forward into my space, pushing me back into my seat with that darn power of his. The kernel inside me unfurled, ruffled and annoyed, and power swelled inside me, shooting out to smack his aura upside the head. *Back the fuck off.*

He sat back, his mouth parted, and then he smiled—a beauteous glorious thing. It transformed his harsh, forbidding face into something entirely … wow. And were those angels singing?

"Where do you need to be, Miss Hunter?"

"Brahma Corp."

The smile evaporated, and his expression sobered.

Aw, no fair.

He pressed the intercom button. "Brahma Corp, please."

The limo peeled away from the curb.

"So, tell me what happened," he said. "The news was sketchy at best."

"Well, these guys wreathed in shadows broke into the clearing and killed everyone. They had these silver weapons that glowed when they made contact with the yaksha. Swords and whips and daggers."

Vritra's eyes narrowed. "And you don't know who they are?"

"Nope."

His eyes lips thinned. “So, you go running to Brahma Corp to speak to a god.”

I shrugged. “Yeah. Why? Wait. Do *you* know what they are?”

He folded his arms across his chest, his expression shuttered.

Seriously? He was going to hold out on me because I hadn’t thought to come to him first? “Oh, come on. I don’t even know you, not like I know Indra and Varuna. Besides, they’re *gods* and you’re a *demi*god.”

“A demigod who saved your pretty, little arse at the Mayfair quarterly ball. A demigod who actually gives a damn whether you live or die. Tell me, did Indra or Varuna contact you after you almost died to see how you were coping? Tell me, exactly how many times have they been in touch since you and your little gang saved the fucking world?” He was spitting mad, like proper vibrating with it. His nostrils flared. “Answer me.”

I sat up straighter, fuck if he was going to see me cower. “No. And zero. But they’re gods, so they’re probably really busy." Yeah, that was lame, even to my ears.

He snorted. "Yeah, they're gods, and they concern themselves only with things that benefit them—your friend Malina, for example. Now, she was important to them. You, on the other hand, were merely covered by proxy."

And now they didn't need us anymore. Had I been naive in thinking they'd help me now? Just drop whatever they were doing and say, hey, yeah, come on up for a chin-wag? Fucking hell. The fire went out of my argument, and the tension drained from my limbs.

I met his gaze. "Can you help me?"

He exhaled, the anger leaving his face. "Damn it, Carmella," he said softly. "It's all I've been trying to do since we met."

If sincerity were an odor, he'd be reeking of it. Why was I running? What was I afraid of? Oh, yeah, the fact that he was one of the suspects in the Ghandarva case. One of the three men who'd known I'd had the dead Ghandarva's feather. I shouldn't trust him, except right now, my gut told me that he was telling the truth.

"Tell me what they are?"

"On one condition," he said.

"What?"

"You agree to come and train with me. Just once or twice a week. Train with me and learn to master your power."

Spend more time in his company, with his aura intruding on mine. The thought sucked the air from my lungs. "Why does it matter to you so much?"

"Because, you're asura, and the asuras are my responsibility. Because I prefer live Carmella to dead Carmella."

My lips twitched. Couldn't argue with that. "Fine. It's a deal. Now tell me what we're dealing with."

He locked gazes with me. "The silver weapons that glow when making contact are only ever carried by one entity—the *amduth*. The reaper."

"A reaper? Yes. Malina told me about those, but they work for Yama, the lord of the Underworld, right? I'm so confused."

"They did. But after the gods closed the gates of hell for the first time, several broke free and went rogue. The 'Thirteen Yamduth of War' they were called. The only reapers to carry weapons. I've heard rumors of them taking on bounty hunting jobs, but from what I heard they were working solo. The Thirteen working together again? Well, that only ever happened in the great wars when there were too many souls to reap."

Supernatural bounty hunters. That made sense. It fit perfectly with Honey's theory. But would a yaksha beta even know how to contact these Yamduth?

"I don't understand how someone would go about recruiting these creatures."

Vritra shrugged. "I'd have to look into it and get back to you. But one thing I can tell you for sure—their weapons are special. They only glow when extracting a soul. The bounty hunter jobs I heard about were straight kills. The souls were left for Yama's reapers. So the question is—what do the Yamduth want with all the yaksha souls?"

5

Vritra dropped me outside Brahma Corp where Honey was waiting. She was leaning against her bright yellow Mini. Charlie, she called it. The thing was an antique, but a damn well maintained one. Honey had a way with engines, and this one loved to purr.

"Was that who I think it was?" she asked.

"Yeah. And he was very informative. Come on. Let me buy you lunch, and I'll fill you in."

"I thought we were going into Brahma Corp." She eyed the building.

"No need now."

"Damn, I've always wanted to see the inside. Speak to a god."

Except now I wasn't so sure that the gods would be bothered to speak to us. Vritra's words, although harsh, had struck a chord. The gods must have known about the lab incident, it was all over the news, and the massacre was huge news, and yet neither Indra nor Varuna had bothered to reach out to see if I needed anything. Vritra was right. I'd been covered by proxy. Would they be as accommodating for Malina now that she was no longer the gatekeeper of hell? It didn't matter. We had the information we needed.

"Maybe some other time." I linked arms with her and steered her away from the building.

We found a small pub that also served food and settled in with cold glasses of lemonade.

"So, what did you find out?" Honey asked.

I told her and then sat back and sipped my drink, mouth dry from talking so much.

"Fucking hell." Honey slumped back in her seat. "What now?"

"We need to find out how someone might summon a yamduth. How do you put out a bounty for the reapers to collect?"

Honey glanced at her watch. "I have the beta meeting in a couple of hours. Well, I should call it the new alpha meeting. They've picked neutral territory, thank goodness. Hired out the Stag and Boar in Finchley for the evening. I'll scope them out. Father took me along to enough meetings in the guise of caterer for me to know how it works. I just … damn, I'm fucking nervous."

"Because you're a woman?"

She snorted. "Yaksha mostly treat their women like commodities. Renegade was different. Is different. You don't get females with the alpha gene, not because they don't exist, but because it gets beaten out of them."

"What do you mean?"

"Exactly that. Potential alpha females are broken, beaten and, in some extreme cases, raped until they're nothing but frightened wrecks. Father did the opposite with me. He declared me his heir and trained me the best he could. Kieran was beta, but we all knew that my alpha gene was stronger than my brother's."

"So how come you weren't beta?"

She shrugged. “I didn’t want it. To be honest, I don’t want to be the alpha either. Kieran and I discussed it. He was meant to take over, not me. Now, I have no choice. There isn’t another yaksha in the pack with an alpha gene dominant enough to take the reins. The other packs aren’t going to take this laying down. Trust me, there’s gonna be a lot of testosterone at the meeting.”

“In that case, how about I come with you? Add some extra estrogen to the mix.”

She shook her head. “It’s too dangerous. Things could get violent.”

“All the more reason to have more back up, right?”

She dropped her gaze.

“Wait, were you going to go alone?”

She shrugged. “The pack is frightened. The strongest members were killed at the gathering. The rest simply want to mourn and get on with it. I couldn’t drag someone with me. This is my duty—to protect them. To prevent our pack being swallowed up by another.”

"So, I'm coming with you. No arguments. Look, it's part of the case. Until we say otherwise, every beta is a suspect. I'll come with you in an official capacity. I need to interview the betas—sorry, new alphas—anyway. Check their whereabouts and movements over the last few weeks."

"Yeah, that'll go down well," she drawled sarcastically.

I shrugged. "It will when I tell them they can either answer my questions in the comfort of the pub on neutral territory or get hauled into the IEPEU and get quizzed in an interrogation room."

She caught her bottom lip between her teeth. "There is one more thing."

"Go on."

"No one really knows about my ability to go full beast. I've never done it in public before. The other night, I just lost it. So …"

"I won't say anything."

"Thank you. It's just, Dad always warned me to keep it under wraps. Yaksha have issues with females having too much power as it is."

The food arrived, and we dug in.

Half an hour later, food all gone, we made our way back onto the street.

Honey led the way to her Mini. "Come on. I'll drop you back at the office so you can fill Murdoch in on what you found out."

"Shit, yeah. Thanks."

"I'll pick you up in an hour for the meeting. You sure you want to come?"

"Definitely."

MURDOCH WAS AT his desk flipping through a case file, a cold cup of coffee—complete with manky skin—at his elbow.

"What did you find out?" he asked, without looking up.

"Yamduth."

"Reapers? Really? No one's ever seen one … well, not seen one and lived to tell the tale."

Was he making a joke? "Yeah, anyway. I'm going to interview all the new alphas later. Find out where they were the night of the massacre, what their movements have been over the last few weeks."

He sat back, his brows low. "And why would you do that?"

"Because they're suspects?"

"Well, that's news to me." He crossed his arms.

Shit, hadn't I told him Honey's theory? Crap. No, I hadn't. So, I filled him in about Honey's conviction and the new alpha meeting, and the frown thawed.

"Yes, it fits. But an interrogation of that magnitude needs to be done in-house. We need to draw up warrants to bring them in for questioning. They won't come willingly."

"Which is why I'm offering them the opportunity to be questioned informally on their territory. Familiar surroundings will help them relax and, hopefully, slip up."

His lips turned down reflectively. "Okay. But you're not going alone."

"No. I'll have the new Renegade Alpha with me."

His brows shot up. "He stepped up quickly."

"*She* had no choice."

He stared at me for a long beat, then nodded. "Take your radio and call for back up if you need. I'll alert dispatch to let them know the situation. Where's the meeting?"

"The Stag and Boar in Finchley."

He made a note. "Be careful, Hunter. Yaksha may look human, but underneath that facade lies a primal beast."

A shiver skittered up my spine. Maybe walking into a room of alphas was a bad idea, but no way was I letting Honey do this alone.

THE YELLOW MINI was parked in the carpark outside the IEPEU. Honey was visible behind the wheel, and there was someone beside her … Victor?

Honey rolled down her window and stuck her head out. "Hunter, over here."

Like I could miss that bright, yellow vehicle.

"Carmella." Victor caught my eye in the rear-view mirror as I climbed in.

"You coming with?"

Victor nodded.

Honey started the engine and backed out of the parking spot. “I popped into the soup kitchen to make my food delivery early and got chatting to Victor. He offered to come with. Well, insisted more like.” She shot him a quick glance, but his eyes were on the road, his expression solemn.

Man, how the hell had he managed to fold his huge body into the Mini? His knees were crushed up against the dash, head pressed against the roof. He looked like even more of a giant in such a confined space.

“The boys are watching the kitchen tonight,” Victor said. “I told Honey she needn’t have brought the food. After what happened, we wouldn’t expect it.”

“No,” Honey said, steering us into traffic toward the North Circular. “Dad wanted to do this. He’d want me to continue to help. I’ve sorted out the staffing at the restaurant Dad was running. It’s fine. I’ll manage.”

“You think the new alphas will have an issue with Victor coming along?”

"Fuck 'em," Victor said.

I balked. Wow, that was the first time I'd heard him curse.

Honey's lips twitched. "Yeah, fuck 'em."

These two, man, there was definitely something going on—some kind of connection.

"One thing though," Honey warned. "Let me do the talking. While you're in there, you're part of my pack, 'kay?"

Part of her pack. "Sure, I can do that. As long as I don't need to bow or scrape."

She chuckled. "Nothing like that. It's just a respect and hierarchy thing. If an alpha can command respect from his pack, then he commands respect from his fellow alphas. Once the meeting is done, I'll hand over the floor to you for the interviews."

We settled into silence, the traffic out the windows speeding by now we were on the main route that wound through the city. My phone buzzed and Banner's name flashed on the screen.

"Hey."

"You could have been killed."

I blew out a breath. "Yeah, I know."

He sighed. “I’m just glad you’re all right. Can I … Can I see you?”

My heart ached. We’d only known each other a short time, but there was a connection. Not the kind he would like, but still. It was probably a bad idea to start spending time with him so soon. There was way too much longing in his voice, but I missed him. So …

“Yeah. I could do with some moral support tomorrow.”

“What’s happening tomorrow?”

Oh, yeah. We hadn’t spoken properly since the night I’d told him we should spend some time apart. “I’m getting cut off from the skein.”

He was silent for a long beat. “I’m sorry, Carmella. I know how much you wanted to be a part of the covens. There’s been some fear and fury over what happened. The smaller covens are the worst, eager to lynch. The Mayfair High Witch made the right call to protect us all.”

“I know.”

“What time is the ceremony?”

“Four.”

"I'll pick you up."

"'Kay."

"See you tomorrow." He hung up with a soft click.

The car swerved as we turned onto a narrow dirt track. Victor mumbled something and Honey snorted.

I peered out the windshield. "The pub is down here?"

"Yep."

Surrounded by woodland in the middle of nowhere. Great. Why had I thought they'd be chilling in the center of town in a quaint British pub? Oh, yeah, the name Stag and Boar. We drove into a clearing strewn with bracken and woodchips. A log cabin-turned-bar glared back at us. Yellow light streamed out from the windows to battle the settling gloom. It swept across the Mini as we came to a halt parallel to the building. Honey killed the engine and we climbed out into the night. Several motorbikes and a couple of trucks were parked up closer to the cabin.

Victor was last to exit, squeezing out, stretching to his full height and cracking his neck.

"Let's get this done," he said.

Yes, let's head into the cabin filled with Yaksha. Heck, what the hell was I scared of? I was standing out here with a rakshasa and a yaksha who could go full beast.

Honey went first, pulled open the door, and stepped into the amber lit interior. Victor stepped aside to let me enter and then followed. His huge bulk was a solid, reassuring presence at my back.

The hum of conversation stalled as soon as we entered. The tables had been pushed together to form a large one, and male yaksha were seated around it, pints in their hands. A couple of bottles of whiskey were set on the table alongside several plates of chicken and ribs, to soak up the alcohol. Not that yaksha needed to soak it up. They burned calories almost as fast as my hellhound friend, Malina.

One of the alphas stood up with a scrape of his chair. "Honey Dante, always nice to see you, but as you can see, we don't require any catering."

Ouch.

Honey stood tall. "Good to see you too, Rohan, and I'm not here to cater."

His gaze flicked over her shoulder to sweep over me and snag on Victor. His eyes narrowed. "What have you brought into our den?"

"For tonight consider them my pack. The Renegade Alpha's pack."

The room broke into murmurs, and Rohan's eyes narrowed. "This is a fucking joke, right?"

A door at the back of the cabin opened and closed, the sound of a toilet flushing trickled out into the bar. Everyone fell silent. The thud of boots was accompanied by a huge yaksha's appearance from the corridor at the side of the bar. He paused to take in the scene, his gaze sweeping over the gathered to land on Honey. He lifted his chin and inhaled, his expression darkening.

Honey tensed. Her right leg twitched as if resisting the urge to take a step back.

Victor growled low in his throat.

"Marco," Rohan said, "this bitch claims she's the new Renegade Alpha."

Marco, the guy by the bar, strode into the room, past the table surrounded by yaksha, and right up to

Honey. Victor moved so fast he was almost a blur. And then he was blocking Marco's access.

Marco chuckled, low and mean. "Back off, Fido. I'm just confirming her story is all."

"It's all right, Victor," Honey said.

Victor stepped back reluctantly.

Marco moved in close enough to touch my friend. He closed his eyes and inhaled, and when he opened them, his pupils had practically eaten away at his gray irises.

Honey cocked her head. "Satisfied?"

"More than. She's alpha all right." He turned to his comrades.

The room erupted in exclamations, growls of disgust, and snorts of displeasure. Yeah, strange how I could distinguish between the two types. I'd been spending way too much time with the monsters.

Marco held up his hand. "Enough!"

The room rumbled into silence, all except for Rohan.

"No way can we have a female alpha."

"Why not?" Honey said, striding up to the table. "You think all we're good for is keeping house and popping out kids?"

His lips curled. "And fucking. You'd be a *real* good fuck."

Victor tensed, his hands balling into fists. Shit, please don't lose your … shit. But it was Marco who diffused the situation.

"She's alpha, Rohan. Deal with it."

"Fuck this!" Rohan stepped away from the table. "I ain't having no meeting with a bitch at the table."

The other alphas murmured in agreement, pushing back seats and stretching to their full heights; the room was suddenly way too small.

"Well, there's an easy way to settle this to everyone's satisfaction," Marco said to Honey. "Your *pack*, against mine. Three on three. What do you say?"

Honey's shoulders tensed, but her tone was lazy, almost bored. "Why? Scared of a little one-on-one?"

Marco chuckled. "Nah, sweetheart. I prefer my one-on-ones with bitches to take place in a bed or up against a wall. Fucking hell, I'd one-on-one you anywhere—but not tonight. You swan in here with your *pack*—these outsiders who know nothing about our ways—and expect a seat at the big boy's table? Well, now you're gonna have to put your money where your mouth is. Let's see if your *pack* is willing to back you up, huh? A friendly brawl. No kill, just disable. What'dya say?"

Rohan grinned cruelly. A couple of the alphas ducked their heads, clearly uncomfortable with the whole thing. But the majority jeered and banged their pint glasses on the table.

Victor could hold his own. Honey must know that. She had to know what he was just by scent, and the yaksha must be able to smell it too. They probably thought he'd be the only threat, discounting Honey and me, and yeah, I'd never fought a yaksha before, but I'd fought guys. Plus, I had an untapped reserve of power inside me eager to come out and play. My tummy fluttered with a twisted sense of anticipation. Honey was hesitating because of me.

No need.

I stepped up behind her. "Do it. Trust me. We can do this."

"Aw, does your little friend want to go home?" Rohan said tauntingly.

Man, how old was he? Five? How could someone so immature ever be alpha? Sucked for his pack.

Honey smiled, slow and deliberate. "Actually, she was wondering how long you guys were gonna stand there showcasing your dicks before we could get on with some good, old-fashioned face pummeling."

Rohan stepped forward threateningly. "Fucking bitch."

"Watch your tongue," Victor said. "Unless you want me to tear it out and feed it to you."

Marco watched us through hooded eyes. "You win, and you get to sit at the table. You lose, and you walk your pretty little arse right out of here and renounce your claim as alpha of the Renegade Pack. You renounce your claim and you merge your pack with Moonlight."

Fucking hell. So, that was his game. He wanted the Renegade Pack. Shit.

He'd backed her into a corner. If she declined, she might as well admit she was too weak to lead, and the other packs would tear at her pack until it was in shreds. If she fought, she risked losing, but she'd go down with honor.

"Outside?" Honey asked.

Marco inclined his head. "Let's do this."

"CARMELLA, YOU SURE about this? I can stop this now," Honey said as we strode out onto the wood chipped lot.

I snorted. "And basically admit you suck as alpha? No. We do this."

Victor shook his head. "Let me have him."

"No. Marco has to be mine," Honey said.

Victor made a sound of exasperation. "I'm glad we don't run in packs. This is pathetic. You're an alpha. They should accept it."

"I'm also a woman. It goes against everything they've been raised to believe." Her smile was hard and determined. "My dad was always a trendsetter.

Now, it's my turn to make sure his legacy stays alive."

The other alphas spilled out onto the cabin decking. Marco, Rohan, and another yaksha I didn't know joined us on the lot.

I leaned in toward Honey. "Wait a second, I thought we were fighting his pack?"

Honey's lips twisted wryly. "He was being figurative. Since you guys are my pack, he's just made up his own."

"Three alphas against one. How the fuck is that fair?"

"It isn't. But yaksha rarely play fair," Honey said. "Spread out. Carmella, I'm so sorry for dragging you into this."

"You can buy me a drink later."

Victor snorted.

Howls rose up into the air, and Marco and his pack charged us.

There was no time to think, only to react. Rohan bee-lined for me, his stocky body primed to take me down. Forget that I was half his size, or that I was a woman, none of that shit mattered, it was written across his feral face. Thank goodness for my IEPEU training, the techniques taught us hand-to-hand combat with supernaturals stronger and faster than us. Most techniques involved shooting it in the face or running. But when those weren't possible, we targeted the ears, eyes, throat, and knees. I braced myself and spun out of the way. He skidded to a halt and came at me again. A short, sharp punch to the soft spot above his kidneys had him gasping in shock. I spun and smashed my fist into his throat, sending him back a step, but fuck he was strong. Trick was not to get pinned. Crap, I was actually doing this, fighting a fucking yaksha. Thank God he hadn't gone all feral. His face rippled, and the beast pressed through, muzzle, fangs, the works. Shit.

Okay. No more punching him in the throat. And going for the eyes was out of the question. That left his knees. A heel to the side of his knee could buckle him but—

"Carmella, watch out!" Honey called, just as Rohan launched himself at me.

He bridged the distance between us in a heartbeat, too fast for me to react, too fast for me to leap out of the way. And then I was down, face pressed to the dirt, his weight on my back. Couldn't move, couldn't breathe. I was done. It was over. Talons scraped against my back, snagging at the waistband of my jeans, yanking, thrusting. What the fuck? What was he …

The howls intensified.

His arousal pressed against my buttocks, and then the seams of my jeans gave way with a terrifying rip.

"No." I writhed under him trying to get free.

"Yes. You like that, don't you?" His breath was hot in my ear. "Fucking makes me hot."

"No!" My roar penetrated the whoosh of blood pounding in my ears.

The kernel inside me exploded and power surged through my limbs: strength, rage, intent. I was on fire with it. Bucking and throwing him off with ease, I advanced on him. The world was a red haze. He picked himself up, his face a mask of confusion and awe.

"No means no!" My voice sounded odd, warped and deep.

I charged and shoved him. He went flying back into the tree line.

"Carmella?" Honey's voice was a strangled whisper.

I turned to find Victor and Honey staring at me. Marco stood to one side, his face a bloody mess, and Victor's opponent was out cold. The world was still tinged red. What was wrong with my eyes?

"Carmella. What the fuck?" Honey glanced down at my arms.

What? I looked down at myself, at the rippling, silver scales that covered my skin, at my elongated talon-tipped hands.

"What the fuck?"

My head grew light. I was gonna—

6

I opened my eyes to an unfamiliar ceiling. The yaksha fight … the scales on my arm. Oh, fuck. I sat up, examining my skin—my normal, non-scaly skin. Thank God.

"Feeling better?" Vritra padded into the room, a towel slung low on his hips, his bare chest glistening with skating droplets of water.

What the … He was naked. Well almost, but, wow. "How did I get here?"

He toweled his hair, watching me carefully. "I carried you to the car, and then we drove the rest of the way."

Shit. He was huge, taut and smooth and bronzed, and no wonder my pulse was doing a canter. Focus, dammit. "Where are Honey and Victor?"

He shrugged. "I have no idea. Your mobile is on the bedside table, so feel free to call them."

"They just let you take me?"

He snorted. "Well, considering you were in the process of going full dragon at the time, they hardly had a choice."

The scales on my arms, the red haze that had fallen over my vision. "I don't understand." Maybe I kinda did. I just didn't want to.

He slid open the huge wardrobe and selected a cream T-shirt and shrugged it on. Then he dropped the towel.

Oh, shitting hell. I slapped my hands over my eyes.

His chuckle reverberated through the air. "Come now, I'm sure you've seen a half-naked male before."

Yeah, but not one hung like *that*. Fucking hell. My ears were on fire. "Look, as much as I'm not enjoying the show, can you please tell me what the heck I'm doing here? What happened to me out there?"

"You can look now."

I dropped my hand to find him lounging by the patio doors in designer jeans and a cream T. He looked younger. Relaxed. Hot.

"You're an asura," he said.

"Yes, I know *that*."

"And all the asuras have an element of the dragon in them. You just seem to have … more."

"Dragons? As in the winged scaly fire breathing creatures?"

He sighed. "Dragons as in the serpent dragons, and yes, some can command fire, turn their skin to armor, but only one could shift fully into that majestic form … until now." His gaze was speculative.

"Who?"

He smiled. "Me. I am the dragon—the bringer of droughts. And you, Miss Hunter, are the only other asura I have come across in a millennium who can take the dragon form. Your friend, Honey, contacted me when you began to shift. By the time I got there, the yaksha had you bound. You were no longer yourself."

"I can't remember."

"No, you wouldn't. It makes sense. Your asura half was locked away for so long you never learned to assimilate with it. In effect, it's become a separate entity with its own consciousness, and today, all it wished to do was protect you."

I had a dragon inside me? The kernel that had exploded when Rohan had tried to … oh, man. "What do I do?"

"You train with me. You learn to master your dragon and tame it. Otherwise, I fear the next time she comes out, even I won't be able to coerce her back into her box."

His ember eyes were bright in his face as they raked over me.

"How did you … *coerce* her back into her box?"

He smirked. "My dragon can be mighty persuasive." Fingers of his power stroked the air an inch from my skin. My breath caught and something inside me shifted. Was that her? The dragon I was housing? Oh, God.

"Why now? Why not when I was being attacked in Soho, or at the Mayfair Mansion, or even at the yaksha gathering? Why is she coming out now?"

He shrugged. "Who knows? Maybe she's finally fully awake, aware, and ready to become a part of this world. She was cocooned and locked away for a long time. She wants to know you. She *is* you."

He sauntered toward me, and his presence, his aura, expanded to push against me until my back was pressed to the headboard, and my breath was stuck in my throat. The kernel inside me unfurled. Power stretching lazily as if waking from a nap. It expanded outward, and oh, fuck. I was touching him … caressing his signature. His aura rubbed against mine … against the dragon inside.

Vritra exhaled sharply and pulled back, his throat working. "Monday evening. I'll send a car for you." His voice was deeper—raspy and almost breathless. "We begin training."

Had the contact affected him as much as it had me? What the heck was going on here? The cuff on my wrist tingled, and my heart rate slowed.

"You're willful, just like your father," Vritra said.

My father? Yes, he'd mentioned him at the IEPEU hospital after I'd survived the attack. But I'd had a dad, a good one. Still, I needed to know. "Who was he?"

"He was my friend. I recall him telling me about a witch he was seeing. He never went into detail, never mentioned it more than a couple of times. I just assumed the liaison fizzled out."

"Where is he now?"

"Dhani was killed in a bar brawl over twenty-five years ago."

So, before I'd been born. "I thought you guys were immortal?"

"Immortal, but not invulnerable. We can still die. Not all asura have super healing abilities or armor skin."

Had Mother known what happened to him? Did she wonder where he was and then think he'd abandoned her? Oh, God, maybe she'd hated me because I was a reminder of him. It still didn't answer the question of who had bound my powers, and there'd be no answers until I found her.

Vritra opened the door. "Exit the suite, and take the lift down to the ground floor. A car will be waiting to take you home." He made to step out of the room. "And Miss Hunter? Try not to get into any scrapes between now and Monday."

He closed the door softly behind him.

For several long seconds I didn't move, expecting the door to open, for him to come sauntering back in, for the tension to fill the air once more and suffocate me with a complicated combination of allure and repulsion. The sheets smelled of him, the room reeked of him—cinnamon and exotic stuff—that made my core ache. I needed to get away. Climbing off the overindulgent bed, I headed to the door, cracked it open, and slipped out into the main suite.

Vritra was nowhere to be seen, the fancy penthouse was immaculate, masculine, and completely empty. The corridor beyond was wide and spacious and another door, probably to a separate suite, faced me. Ducking out of Vritra's room, I headed toward the lift at the end of the white carpeted corridor. The doors swished open as I approached to reveal a svelte female figure.

Henna.

"What the hell are you doing here?" She barreled toward me, all rage and indignation.

No, I was done being attacked. The power inside me surged up, simmering under my skin. "Back the fuck off!"

Henna froze, her chest rising and falling as she assessed me. But sod that, I was done being assessed. I wanted my sofa, slippers, and a bucket of chow mein. I pushed past her, stepped into the lift, and jabbed my thumb against the ground floor button. She turned to face me, and the doors slid shut on her horrified face.

7

"Thank god you're safe." Honey stepped into the flat and pulled me into a hug. "I didn't know what to do. You were all *grrr*, and the other yaksha were freaking out, then Victor mentioned your asura side, and the only person I could think to call was Vritra. Thank God you had his number in your phone."

I hugged her back. "It's okay, you don't have to explain. You did the right thing. Thank you."

"You want a glass of wine?" Urvashi offered from her perch on the floor by the sofa. She'd beat Honey by two minutes, and the bottle was already opened. That woman was a ninja with a corkscrew.

"God, yes." Honey released me and parked her butt on the sofa-bed.

I closed the door and joined them. No alcohol for me though. There was a dragon inside me, and alcohol loosened inhibitions. I had the feeling that right now my inhibitions were integral to keeping the power inside in its box.

"So, what happened with Vritra?" Honey asked.

"Well, he wandered around his bedroom half naked for the first part, which was kind of a distraction."

Urvashi spat out her wine. "The fuck?"

"No fucks. Just talking."

She wiped at her mouth and smiled slyly. "But you wanted to, right?"

"No. I didn't want to do … *that*. I was confused and scared."

"And distracted," Honey added.

"Fine, the guy is hot. But he's also uber intense and scary. No. I just can't go there." Paimon's face flashed in my mind, and I archived the image, just like all the rest that kept popping up in my head. He was betrothed for godsake. Get over it.

"So, did Vritra explain what happened to you?" Honey asked.

I filled them in best I could, but left out the parts about our powers rubbing up against each other.

Urvashi let out a low whistle. “Wow. That’s something. Vritra has been the only one of his kind for a long time; no wonder he was attracted to you. He could probably sense what you were even though he didn’t know it.”

“I guess.”

“So, you gonna train with him?” Honey asked.

“I don’t have much choice. I can’t risk losing control like that again. I could’ve hurt someone.”

Honey nodded. “Yeah, you really could have. It took eight yaksha to pin you and tie you up, and then you started to get all scary and huge. Kinda like the Hulk but with scales.”

Shit. “I’m so sorry. I completely messed up your meeting.” The interviews! How was I was going to explain this to Murdoch?

Honey snorted. “Actually, you did me a favor. After watching you go all she-Hulk, they were more than willing to give me a seat at the big boys’ table. Not sure how long it will last but …” She shrugged.

“Any ideas on who might have placed the hit?”

Honey's smile fell. "No. They're all bastards. Could have been any one of them."

"Although Marco's comment about taking over Renegade flags him as a possible prime suspect."

Urvashi topped up her glass. "I vote we hit pause on the doom and gloom for the evening. Tomorrow is gonna be a shitty day cos Carmella is getting the snip. So, I say we get pissed and talk about sex."

I rolled my eyes. "Do you have to put it like that?"

She grinned. "Fuck 'em. Let them keep their skein. You've got a dragon. Seriously, Carmella, to be an asura with that power, that ability—it's huge."

It was also a world I wasn't sure I wanted to be a part of. I'd always been a witch-blood. Even without the power, that name had given me a community, an identity. And now that identity was being stripped away. Sure, the asuras would adopt me, Vritra would make sure of it, but what guarantee was there that they'd *want* me? That one slip, one deficiency wouldn't get me cut off from their world? Best to stay in between. Urvashi, Honey, Banner, and Victor were my tribe. The covens could go suck it. And once I'd learned how to control the dragon inside me, the asuras could suck it too.

"I prefer being an independent agent." I winked. "IEPEU and you guys, that's all I need."

Honey and Urvashi exchanged a glance I couldn't quite decipher.

Someone knocked at the door.

Urvashi made to get up.

Waving her back down, I hauled my ass up to answer it.

"Surprise!" Aunt Constance held out her arms.

She was back. The woman who'd picked up the pieces of me and super glued them back together. She was back, and my heart swelled with joy. The tide of emotion I'd been holding back for weeks came surging to the surface, and my vision blurred.

Aunt's brow furrowed, and then I was in her arms, pressed to her bosom.

THE SMELL OF freshly baked croissants and coffee woke me. Aunt Constance smoothed back the hair from my forehead.

"Up and at 'em, girl. Big day today. The beginning of a new chapter in your life." She said the words in a sing-song voice.

Time for the snip. I sat up, rubbing sleep from my eyes. "You got croissants. I love croissants."

"I know. I had Urvashi send them up. Water's hot, go jump in the shower."

Man, I loved that woman. She always knew what to say and how to kick my arse into gear. I'd missed her so much.

"Aunt, I'm sorry. You shouldn't have to come back to all this drama."

She pressed her lips together. "No. You shouldn't have to be going through this. If I'd known … Damn your mother. When I get hold of her …"

"You know where she might be?"

Aunt nodded. "There're a few places she might go. Leave it to me. I'll find her. She needs to be made accountable for what's happened to you, and trust me, we *will* get answers. Now, up you get. Shower, eat, and get your day started. You're more than a witch blood. You're more than an asura. You're Carmella Hunter, my wonderful, kind, generous, and incredibly brave niece. And don't you forget it."

There was no arguing with my aunt. And I loved it.

WE CRUNCHED UP the drive to the Mayfair Mansion in Banner's fancy car.

His profile was serious and concerned, but it was him I was worried about. "Are you sure it's okay for you to come with me?"

"No," he said. "But if they want me to leave, they're going have to throw me out." The corner of his mouth lifted in a cocky smile. "And I'd like to see them try."

Aw, now I had the warm-fuzzies but still. "Don't get into a scrape over me. I'm a big girl. You don't need to hold my hand." *Please, hold my hand. Please.*

He parked outside the elaborate entrance. "I know. But I want to. So, shut it."

If someone had told me three weeks ago I'd end up being friends with Mal Banner, I'd have had them committed. But here we were. Friends. Or as close to it as we could be.

He killed the engine and turned to look at me. "I wish there was some other way." His chest rose and fell with a heavy sigh. "I really do."

He sounded so sad, so end of the world. I punched him lightly on the arm. "Hey, it's just magick. I can live without it."

He blew out a breath and nodded. "Yes, of course." He grinned. "Fuck it, right?"

"Right."

The house loomed above us, forbidding and judgmental. Urgh, stop it. It was just a building. A building in which I was about to get an essential part of me removed. Up the steps and through the doors we went. And there she was, the High Witch, waiting to greet me. Her smile dropped at the sight of Banner.

"Mr. Banner, how nice of you to give Miss Hunter a lift."

Banner's jaw tightened. "Let's cut the crap. I'm staying."

The High Witch's left eye twitched, and then she exhaled through her nose. "This isn't your domain, Mal. You know this isn't how things are done. You don't belong here."

"And in a few minutes, neither will Carmella. So, I think she has the right to have a friend with her when you take away her identity."

The High Witch's brows snapped together. "You speak as if we have a choice. You know as well as I that this is the only way to protect her from the coven's wrath, and if I recall correctly, it was the Piccadilly Coven that bayed for blood the loudest when we met to discuss this very issue."

Banner's lips tightened. "The coven does not speak for me."

"No, I can see that. Very well. Stay if you must, but keep your peace. This is a delicate spell. The intent must be pure."

Banner's shoulders relaxed.

She led us past the staircase, through a mahogany furnished sitting room, and down a long corridor toward the back of the house. Several arches and closed doors later, we stopped outside a plain black door.

"Now Carmella, this room may look daunting to you, but it is merely ceremonial. Do not be frightened."

"Um … okay."

Banner snorted. "Do you have to do the whole robe thing?"

The High Witch glared at him, her eyes flashing dangerously. "One more word from you, and I will forget your status and expel you from the premises."

Banner snapped his mouth closed.

We stepped into a huge circular chamber with a domed glass ceiling. The floor was tiled and etched with strange symbols. A raised circular platform, with twelve robed figures standing on it, ran around the circumference of the room. The figures' faces were obscured by deep hoods. The High Witch left my side and strode across the floor. She climbed up onto the podium and picked up something from the ground—a robe. She shrugged it on. Her gaze locked with mine, and then she inclined her head, raising the hood to hide her face.

Banner leaned in to whisper in my ear. “You need to stand in the circle.”

Ah, okay. I walked into the center of the room. Now what?

The High Witch’s voice filled the room. “Carmella Hunter, you have been charged with disrupting the natural fabric of the skein. You are an abomination that must not be allowed to continue to taint the sacred skein.”

What the fuck? Abomination? Heat stirred in the pit of my belly.

“Your sentence is final. To be cut off. To be banished. A witch no longer.”

The other robed witches joined in. “To be cut off. To be banished. A witch no longer.”

My scalp prickled, and the room grew dark as rainclouds swept over us, blocking the sun’s rays. A shiver ran up my spine, and the witches began to hum.

The sound vibrated in my teeth and bones, and the kernel inside me pulsed in agitation. Then there was the skein, glowing brightly in my mind, alive and connected to me, to my heart. Not just one thread but several, buried deep inside me.

The hum intensified, and the threads began to vibrate and shiver. It was happening, whatever they were doing was working. I didn't want this. I couldn't do this. Those threads were a part of me, they belonged to me.

One by one, they went dark.

"No." I fell to the ground, a hollow ache swelling inside me. It was gone. My connection was gone, and in its place was a void.

The kernel unfurled and warmth spread through my limbs, seeping into the void left by the absence of my connection to the skein. It was a hug from my dragon—an it's-all-right-you-still-have-me.

The clouds parted, and a ray of sun lanced down into the room, placing me in the spotlight.

"Carmella?" Banner helped me off the floor.

My legs were rubbery, my insides quivering as if recovering from the flu. My asura power swelled, dispelling the symptoms, and my mind was suddenly clear. They'd called me an abomination. My eyes grew hot, not with sorrow, but with anger. I shook

Banner off and stood tall, my gaze fixed on the robed figure of the High Witch.

"Thanks for that. Thanks for spelling out just what I am to the covens—an abomination. Well this *abomination* is no longer your problem, and your problems are no longer mine." I pulled the pearl from my pocket and held it up. "Catch your own damned Daayan." I lobbed it at her, turned on my heel, and stormed out of the room.

I was done with the covens. Done with their magick.

It was time for me to start fresh.

Time to learn what being an asura was all about.

8

"Did you get a look at her face when you lobbed the pearl at her?" Urvashi asked, leaning across the table.

"She had the damned hood on, so no."

We were seated in a corner booth in my favorite bar, Bottoms Up, in Leicester Square. It was a quaint place with a sixties-themed decor. Even the staff dressed up, and the drinks all had funny names based on sixties fashion. After the spell at the Mayfair Mansion, I'd had Banner drop me here and called the girls. We'd been hanging out ever since. Eating, drinking, and just trying to feel better about shit that happened. My pain was nothing compared to Honey's, but then Honey was something else—focused, determined, and strong. Her family was dead, but she was taking care of business. But then, like she'd said, she didn't have the luxury of falling apart. I just hoped she allowed herself time to grieve. Holding it in like that, burying it … it couldn't be healthy.

Honey shoved a handful of peanuts into her mouth, and chewed. "Fuck 'em. You're better off."

"Yeah." My stomach felt hollow. "I start training with Vritra tomorrow evening."

Urvashi slapped the table. "Good on you."

"You think they'll come at you for the Daayan thing?" Honey asked.

I shrugged. "I don't care. I'm done being blamed for stuff out of my control, punished and used. They can figure out how to catch her themselves."

"But what if she comes for you?"

Yeah, the thought had crossed my mind. The pearl had been my only protection, but what was done was done. "If she comes for me, then she'll have a fight on her hands."

If my asura power wasn't under control by then, I'd call on Paimon. But there was no way I was asking the coven for anything *ever* again.

Honey got up. "What you ladies having this round?"

How many rounds had that been? Five? Six? So much for avoiding alcohol. But the dragon was sleeping in its box, and I didn't feel at all tipsy. Maybe being asura meant I couldn't get drunk?

"I'll have a Baby Doll," Urvashi said.

"Capri for me."

Honey wandered off to the bar, her jean-clad arse swaying and catching the eye of every male in the room. I swept my gaze back to Urvashi and caught a woman's eye. She was seated by the window, alone. Her long, dark hair was pulled back from her face and braided. She averted her gaze and turned her head to look out of the window.

Had she been watching us?

"Hey? What you looking at?" Urvashi turned in her seat to follow my gaze.

I drained my glass. "Nothing. Thought the woman by the window was watching us."

Urvashi frowned. "What woman?"

"The one over …" She was gone. "Never mind."

Honey returned with our drinks, and the sixth or seventh round commenced.

An hour later, the place was heaving with the night-life crew. Did Sunday nights mean nothing to some people? Heck, what was I talking about? This was London.

A group of guys spotted us and started to wind their way over.

"Time to leave ladies." I scooted out of the booth, and we headed for the door. Outside, the cool breeze was refreshing against my warm skin.

"We should call a taxi," Urvashi said. "Carmella, your flat is closest, can we crash with you?"

Honey giggled. "On her teeny tiny sofa-bed? Cozy."

"Hey, that sofa-bed is mighty comfy."

We clipped arm in arm down the lamp-lit street. Well not clipped, because none of us were wearing heels. Urvashi was dressed breezily in a short sundress and Hercules sandals, and Honey was wearing cut-off jeans and ballet flats similar to mine. The streets were still buzzing with life.

Someone screamed.

"Nope. No, no, no." Urvashi shook her head, hair swishing. "Not tonight."

Several more screams joined the first. We were walking toward the shouts and yells and then the reason for the panic was striding toward us.

Honey tensed. "Motherfucker."

Urvashi's grip on my arm tightened. "What … what are they?"

"Yamduth." And they were headed right for us.

Honey shoved us away from her. "Run, get the fuck out of here. It's me they want."

Her body vibrated, and her face began to morph. More screams erupted around us, whether at the site of the silver weapons the two Yamduth were carrying, or the fact that a yaksha was shifting in the street right in front of them.

The power inside me stirred. "Fuck that, we do this together."

"Wait." Urvashi said. "Let me distract them, you run."

"What?"

But then she opened her mouth and began to sing. The melody that spilled forth was the likes of nothing I'd ever heard before. The screams died, and the Yamduth faltered. Urvashi stepped in front of us, moving sinuously toward the reapers. They watched her, eyes glazing over.

"We can't just leave her," Honey said.

But I'd seen the ancient being in Urvashi's eyes. She had this under control. I needed to protect Honey. Whoever had put a hit on the yaksha obviously wanted Honey out of the way too. After all, she'd been the only yaksha left standing at that gathering. This was either a finish-the-job scenario, or a get-rid-of-the-female-yaksha bid. Either way, Honey's life was at stake.

"Go. Now." I shoved her. "I'll stay with Urvashi. It's not me they're after."

Honey took a step back, and a deep rumble cut through Urvashi's song. It was coming from the Yamduth. They were shaking. No. Not shaking. They were laughing.

Urvashi's melody faltered and died. She glanced over her shoulder at us just as the nearest yamduth lashed out, backhanding her and sending her flying through the window of the restaurant to our left.

Honey roared and charged.

"NO!" I bolted after her. My power rose to infuse my limbs with uncanny strength, but Honey was already within reach of the killers. Except … they weren't paying her any attention. Their attention was fixed on me.

Honey cut an arch through the air from a backhand delivered by the second yamduth.

I skidded to a halt.

Me … They wanted me? "What the—"

"Carmella, run!" Urvashi screamed.

My feet acted on instinct, and I was off, running down the street, weaving and bumping into late night revelers. Horns honked and screams lit up in my wake. They were right on my tail. Fuck! The power within me tugged and flared, wanting to be free. *She* wanted to be free, to fight. But I couldn't let her out, not here, not with all these innocent people about. Someone could get hurt. The yamduth weren't interested in anyone else, they wanted me. If I could lead them somewhere less populated? Hah, less populated in the center of London? What a joke.

The neon lights of the club district blinked up ahead. Shit, shit, shit. There was nowhere to go. The dragon within me stretched, ready to burst from my itching skin.

My heart was beating too fast. I couldn't control her. Oh, God.

Please, you can't come out here. Don't come out. Just help me.

The power snorted—hot plumes of smoke.

Please.

Pain skated across my skin, prickling and stabbing like a thousand needles. There'd be crowds of people up ahead—tourists to the city—innocent humans.

Stop. It was time to stop.

I ground to a halt and turned to face the reapers. They slowed their pace, coming to a stop a meter or so away. Both carried silver swords that gleamed in the moonlight. Their eyes glowed eerily from within the shadows that shifted across their faces and swirled around their bodies.

I crouched, hands raised in a fighting stance. Silver glinted off my skin—my iridescent scales. My armor.

Thank you.

The power inside settled over me, rippling over my body, ready to protect the heck out of me. Could their weapons cut through dragon hide?

They must be thinking the same thing, because they weren't attacking. Not yet.

"Come on! If you want me, you're going to have to come and get me." Damn it mouth, shut the heck up. There were eyes on us, watching the scene. Humans out for a good time were now taking in an impromptu show. Fucking hell, just get on with it already.

Attack.

The urge was so strong I had to tense my calves not to comply, and then my fingertips were on fire as they gave birth to wicked sharp talons.

Oh, shit.

My vision started to blur, and a red tinge closed in. No, please don't take over.

Attack.

This time, there was no denying the command. I lunged at the yamduth, lashing out with my talons and swiping away the shadows surrounding them to catch a glint of gold on bronze flesh. A sword arched toward me, and I rolled out of the way, coming up just as the other yamduth sliced with his weapon. Shit. I brought my arm up to shield my face. The sword made contact with a scrape and flash of embers. Fucking hell. Yes!

"Carmella!"

Honey and Urvashi ran past the Yamduth to stand by me. Ready to take on the reapers if need be.

"Come on! What are you waiting for?"

They didn't attack though. Instead, they began to back away. Scared? No. Just at a loss as to how to kill an asura with impenetrable skin. The shadows around them began to whirl faster and faster. They were going to get away.

Attack.

But what was the point? I couldn't kill them. They were smoke and shadow. We needed more information. How *did* you kill a reaper?

“Who sent you? What did you do with the Yaksha souls? Answer me, dammit!”

The shadows condensed, curled up, and winked out. The Yamduth were gone.

“Oh, God.” Urvashi doubled over, hands on her knees.

“They wanted to kill *you*,” Honey said. “Why? Why you?”

“I don’t know.” But I sure as hell was gonna find out.

9

The journey back to the flat was … eventful. People snapping photos and taking videos of the freak with scales for skin walking though the town, because no matter how hard I tried, I couldn't get the scales to just go away. I was armored, head to toe. My face … oh, man. I didn't even want to think about it.

Honey had to leave when we got back—pack business—but Urvashi stayed while we waited for Vritra to show up.

"How much longer is he going to be?" I paced the room.

"Well, unless he can teleport, at least thirty minutes. We only called him a quarter of an hour ago."

A knock at the door. Urvashi jumped up. "Maybe he *can* teleport."

She answered the door, and Banner came spilling into the flat. He stopped short at the sight of me.

"So, it's true."

I stood hands on hips. "How the heck did you know?"

"It's all over the internet. The fight with the Yamduth and then you … changing."

"Great, now I'm a celebrity."

"The videos have gone viral."

"Urgh. Kill me now."

"Kinda impossible since you have impenetrable skin," Urvashi said.

"Really? You mean they couldn't hurt you at all?" Banner asked.

"Yeah."

He blew out a breath. "But that's good, right? Great, in fact."

"Yep, you can't see it, but I'm dancing for joy inside."

Banner pressed his lips together. "No need to be sarcastic. I nearly had a heart attack when I saw that video and realized it was you."

Gah, these scales were making me testy. "I'm sorry."

"I don't understand why they're after you though? It makes no sense," Banner said. "I thought this was a hit on the Yaksha."

"Yeah, so did I."

"Unless …" Urvashi said. "Unless this is a different hit. A new hit. The Yamduth are mercenaries for hire right?"

"But who would want me dead? I mean, why?"

Urvashi raised her brows. "Seriously? Who did you chuck a pearl at and pretty much tell to go fuck herself? You refused the Daayan job."

Banner rubbed a hand over his face. "No, I can't believe the Mayfair coven would stoop to this."

The High Witch had said she was protecting me from the coven's wrath by cutting off my magick, but maybe my denying the Daayan job had pissed someone off. But wrath didn't mean kill, right? Because if they killed me, they'd lose the only person who could put the Daayan back where she belonged. They were going to need me once they found her. Dead Carmella was a useless Carmella. And yeah, I'd help, because this was bigger than my hurt at being labeled an abomination.

I shook my head. "No. It's not the covens. They need me alive to send the Daayan possessing Karen back—once they find her, of course."

Banner sighed. "They're working on it." He reached into his pocket and pulled out the pearl. "The High Witch asked me to give this to you for your protection. As much as you may not like it, the Daayan will most likely come for you. And as hard as the coven is scrambling to trace her, the truth is that you're the only one who can send her back where she belongs." He shrugged. "It's important to the high witches, not only to free Karen, but I get the impression it's something to do with the balance of power and the skein. But no one in the upper ranks is talking."

Of course, he didn't know the truth. About the bargain the thirteen original witches had made with the demon, or the price they'd paid for it. He didn't know that the Daayan were the vengeful souls of thirteen innocent women offered in sacrifice to the demon. He didn't know the Daayan were from the thirteen original witch bloodlines. And as much as I'd like to, I couldn't tell him. I was bound by a witch's oath. Even though my connection to the skein was suppressed, my genetics still screamed witch.

I had no choice but to accept the pearl, really. My anger wasn't justification enough for innocent people to be hurt by whatever this demon doled out if he didn't get his Daayan back.

"If she comes for me, I'll trap her."

Banner nodded. "Good. You know what? The armor skin … It's beautiful."

"Yeah, right." Thank goodness you couldn't blush through scales.

Another knock at the door. This had to be Vritra.

Urvashi let him in, and the room was instantly too small. Banner looked from me to Vritra.

I smiled to soften my next words. "Thank you for coming over to check on me. I'll let you know how I get on with the Daayan thing."

Banner's expression shuttered. "If you need help with anything, call me." He skirted around Vritra and strode out of the door.

Urvashi gathered her things. "I'm going to get going. Call me later."

The door closed behind her, leaving me alone with Vritra. Nervous excitement bubbled up in the pit of my belly.

"There's a hit on you," he said, his voice a low rumble.

"Yeah, I kinda figured that out."

"You're coming with me."

This again? "No. I'm not. I have a life, friends, shit that I need to get done. I am not running and hiding from a bunch of reapers who can't actually hurt me."

"And what if they send someone else? Someone with a weapon that *can* cut through your armor?"

Whoa, now that was a worrying thought. "There's a weapon like that?"

Vritra sighed. "There's always something, Miss Hunter, and if someone wants you dead badly enough, they will find it. It's unlikely but not impossible."

There was a hit, not denying that, and, yeah, Vritra was right. The person who'd hired the yamduth might find a weapon to hurt me. They would most likely come after me again. But fuck 'em, let them come. I wasn't running. This flat, my friends—they were my life, and I wasn't letting fear of what might happen take them away from me.

I placed my hands on my hips. "A lot of things could happen. If I worried about all the possibilities I may as well lock myself in a steel box and never come out."

Vritra sighed. "Stubborn woman."

"Overbearing man."

We faced off casually, because, you know, I was tired and stuff. "So, can you do your thing and make these go away?"

He was studying me carefully. "Do they cover you under your clothes?"

I swallowed. "Yes."

"Beautiful." The word was a soft exhale.

Oh, man. Was it hot in here? “Look, just get rid of them. Please.”

“You’ve tried to communicate with the power?”

Doh. “Of course, I have. Do you think I would have called you all the way across town if I could do this myself?”

He shrugged off his jacket, unbuttoned the cuffs on his shirt, and rolled them up to expose his bronzed forearms. “Women do a lot of strange things to get me alone.”

I rolled my eyes. “Arrogant much?”

“Incompetent much?”

That stung. “You know this isn’t my fucking fault.”

“Well, you got the power to protect you, so you *can* communicate with it and get it to comply. Question is, why are you failing at retracting the dragon skin? You asked, and the power ignored you. Why is that?”

“I don’t bloody know. Because it hates me? It’s playing games.”

“Your dragon doesn’t play games when it comes to your survival, Miss Hunter. Your survival means *its* survival. So, try again. It complied with your cry for help, so why isn't it complying with you now?"

"I. Don't. Know."

"How does it make you feel? The dragon skin?"

Like a freak, a monster … no, those were projections of what others may think. Think Carmella. I'd almost been killed, and the armor had saved me. Saved me … It made me feel safe and protected. The penny dropped.

I met Vritra's gaze. "Lack of conviction. It knows I still need it. It knows I still need to feel safe."

Vritra smiled. "Your asura power and dragon are connected, and when you are in sync with them, they will give you what you need, even when you don't consciously realize it."

"I'm in sync?"

His lips twitched. "For now. It's a positive step. Now the threat has been averted."

"But they're still out there. They want to kill me."

"Yes. But for now you're safe." He took a step toward me and then another.

The dragon inside lurched in his direction. Tendrils of his power snaked around me, cocooning me in an ethereal embrace.

"You're safe now, Miss Hunter." His voice was a low vibration.

Yes. Yes, I was safe. I exhaled, letting go of the tension that had my muscles in knots. My knees wobbled and then gave way. Vritra caught me neatly and lowered me onto the sofa. He crouched in front of me, his huge frame dwarfing mine. He could crush me with that body. Cover me completely.

"Look." He ran a finger down my arm—my totally non-scaly arm. "All better."

I raised my gaze to look into his face. This close, his eyes were mesmerizing molten orbs. His thick, dark lashes twitched as he scanned my face before locking gazes with me. His power was still surrounding me, cradling me, but then the sensation changed into something else, something akin to a caress up and down my back. Fingers of power slid into my hair and massaged my scalp. Oh, wow. A low moan escaped my lips, and my head fell back, exposing my throat. His body shifted closer, and his heat pressed against me. I wanted to curl into him, press against him and become one.

My mobile buzzed across the coffee table. Whoa, what the heck was I thinking? I jerked back and Vritra sighed.

"You insist on fighting this."

"This?"

"The attraction between us."

I was still throbbing from the head massage. "There is no attraction."

He reached out and cupped my cheek. I couldn't breathe, couldn't move. I wanted to shrug him off, but no, actually I didn't. I wanted to nuzzle his hand. Dammit. What was wrong with me? The man was overbearing and just too cosmic. Being around him made my chest ache with equal parts longing and anxiety. And then he ran his thumb over my bottom lip, and my tongue flicked out to taste him. My ears heated. I'd licked him. What the heck?

His eyes lit up, and a slow smile curled his lips.

He released me and stood, towering over me. "Sleep well, Miss Hunter. I'll see you tomorrow evening for a little one-on-one." He strode to the door and let himself out.

The tension thrumming in the room immediately dissipated, and I slumped back onto the bed.

Something was happening inside me—strange and new and powerful. It was more than the asura power, more than the dragon. It was an awakening, and it knew what it wanted … I just … I wasn't there yet.

MURDOCH LOOKED UP at me from behind his Clark Kent spectacles. "You didn't get the interviews?"

"No. Sorry. It got late and the yaksha were getting antsy."

His gaze narrowed. "And this had nothing to do with your new ability, right?"

Urgh, of course he'd seen the viral video. I grabbed the nearest chair, pulled it up, and sat down. "Look, it won't happen again. I have it under control now." Or would after a few training sessions.

Murdoch shrugged. “You’re not the only one with hidden talents in this place, Hunter. We all have our crosses to bear. Don’t beat yourself up about it. And if we’re going to work together on this case, you need to be honest with me.”

“Okay, I can do that.”

“Who were the Yamduth after in that video? It looked like they were gunning for you.”

I swallowed. “Yeah, they were.”

“Any idea why? Pissed off any influential dangerous people lately?”

“No one that would want me dead.”

“Are you sure?”

The witches needed me alive. “Yes.”

He tapped his pen on the desk. “Okay. I’ll speak to warrants and get them to draw up papers to bring the new alphas in for questioning ASAP. We can split the interviews then knock heads on what we find.”

“Sounds like a plan.”

“We need to figure out if these attacks are related. Right now, it seems unlikely. If the hit was related to taking over the reins in the packs, then it’s very unlikely that the second hit against you has anything to do with that. You're not safe, Hunter. We need to get a detail on you."

As lovely as the extra protection sounded, I knew how stretched we were when it came to boots on the ground. A detail would cost manpower. Manpower we didn't have. "I'm fine. They can't hurt me."

"Ah, yes, your armored skin. Pretty impressive. Still, I'd feel better if we had some operatives looking out for you. I'll see what I can do about getting someone assigned to your case."

"I'm a case now?"

"Yeah. You landed on my desk this morning."

"I'm your case?"

He shrugged. "I guess they figured since we were working together already on one Yamduth attack case, we may as well take the other one too."

"Well, I have no leads. No idea who'd want me dead."

"Leave that to me." He grabbed a notepad and pen and slid them across the desk to me.

"What's this for?"

"Make a list of all your close friends, relatives, and anyone you've had an altercation with in the last two months."

"Why two months?"

"Because most people don't wait more than eight weeks to exact revenge, not unless they're a psychopath playing the long game, and if that's the case, then we're dealing with a whole new ball game."

Great. "I get why you need names of people I've had issues with, but friends and family? What's that about?"

He gave me an indulgent smile. "Oh, Hunter. You reveal your naivety. Don't tell me, you look for the best in people, right? See the smile and take it at face value?"

"Well … um, yeah."

His smile dropped. And his expression hardened. "Well, I don't. I search for the dirt. Burrow until I find the juicy rotten center of a person—the real person beneath the mask. That's where the truth lies. Not in the platitudes and pretty smiles. You'll be surprised how many cases were solved by looking inside a victim's friend circle and not outside. The people that know us best are usually the ones that can hurt us the most effectively."

Well, that explained his hundred percent success rate. "Well, that attitude may work for you, but I prefer not to look at my friends with suspicion. They're my family. My tribe. I'd trust them with my life."

His smile was cynical "In that case, you're lucky you have me to suspect them for you. Now, make the damned list."

As much as I loathed doing it, I grabbed a notepad and began to jot down names. Murdoch was the best investigative officer, and if anyone could figure out who'd ordered the hit on me, it would be him.

Let's just hope I lived long enough for him to find out.

10

The Shaitan Enterprises lobby was buzzing with activity. People flitted to and fro, lifts pinged open and slid shut—the entertainment industry was booming. Whereas Brahma Corp specialized in technological advancement, Shaitan Enterprises focused on anything with entertainment value: cinemas, television, radio, theatre, and music. You name it, and Shaitan Enterprises had their fingers all over it. The reception desk was attached to a set of barriers that stopped unauthorized access to the lifts to the left and right of it. Behind the desk was an open seating area and, beyond that, two golden lifts, sans call button. Those were the lifts I'd spilled out of after my penthouse stay. They must be access panel only, for private use by the residents of the building—Vritra and his asura.

A man strutted out of a lift to my left, tall and lithe, and oh, my God, I knew that face. He'd been plastered all over the silver screen for the past two years. Michael Lion was Midas when it came to the film industry. Every movie he starred in was a blockbuster, and it looked like he was agented by Shaitan Enterprises.

Nice.

He walked past without even giving me a second look. Now normally, I'd be offended, but this guy was into guys, so if he had ogled, I'd have been worried. The receptionist was tapping away furiously at her keyboard.

I leaned against the desk. "Hi."

She stopped typing and looked up with a sunny smile. "How can I help you today?"

Well that was perky. "I have an appointment with Vritra."

She blinked at me. "You mean Mr. Ajagar."

Was that his surname? "Yeah, we can go with that."

"And your name?"

"Carmella Hunter."

She scanned her screen. "I'm sorry. I can't see you in his diary."

Crap. He probably hadn't put the meeting in the diary. "Look, it's not that kind of meeting. He asked me to come and train with him."

She arched a brow. "Mr. Ajagar asked you to *train* with him? Train doing what?"

Okay, I got it. She was just doing her job. I'd be just as skeptical in her shoes if some woman strolled in and claimed she had a training session with the CEO of the company.

"Can you please just call up and let him know I'm here?"

She pressed her lips together. "I'm sorry, but Mr. Ajagar's diary is marked as unavailable for the evening."

Passersby were staring at me now.

"Yes, because he's supposed to be training me." This was getting me nowhere. "You know what, forget it. I'll call him myself." Pulling my phone from my pocket, I dialed Vritra. It rang once and he answered.

"Carmella. Where are you?"

"In the lobby, but you seem to have forgotten to add our appointment to your diary."

He cursed. "Wait there."

The receptionist was watching me closely. Probably thought I was faking the call. A minute passed and then another. The receptionist arched a brow. Hurry up, Vritra.

The golden lifts opened, and Vritra strode out. He was dressed for sparring: yoga pants, a vest, and slippers that could be shucked off easily for the mat.

The receptionist followed my gaze, her back straightened, and she opened her mouth to speak, probably to apologize.

"It's fine, Fanny," Vritra said. "Not your fault. I should have called down to let you know Miss Hunter would be meeting me. I'll be adding her to unrestricted personnel shortly so she'll have an access card to the private lifts."

Fanny nodded. "Yes, Mr. Ajagar."

Vritra waved me over. And with a reassuring smile at the receptionist to show no hard feelings, I followed.

He pressed his palm to the panel by the lift. It opened, and we stepped inside.

"You're hardly dressed for sparring," he said.

The doors slid shut.

"I didn't realize we'd be sparring. I thought you were going to train me in controlling the power inside me."

"And sparring is essential to the training."

"Well, you could have said."

"I believe I told you we'd be having a little one-on-one."

The doors opened into a huge room laid out with mats and ropes and all kinds of obstacle-like equipment. A crowd of males and females were gathered in the center of the room, cheering and calling out encouragement.

I looked up at Vritra. "What's going on?"

"A sparring match. Come." He strode forward, and, as if sensing his presence, the crowed parted to reveal the two fighters on the mats in the center.

I didn't recognize the man, but the woman was all too familiar. Henna flipped the guy and then made to punch him in the throat, stopping short a hairbreadth from his Adam's apple. The crowd whooped.

"How many is that?" a woman to my right said.

"Five out of five," someone replied.

Henna straightened, a playful grin plastered on her face. She caught sight of Vritra and stood straighter, and then her gaze fell to me and her grin dropped. The guy she'd beaten leaped up and slapped her on the back.

"One more. Come on. I know I can beat you."

Henna shrugged him off, jerking her head in our direction. The room went silent as everyone turned to look at me.

Great. Welcome to the freak show, people.

And then the guy on the mats threw up his hands. "Fine. I'll go first, shall I? Hey, my name is Kiran, and you were fucking awesome in the video."

The other asuras all began speaking at once. Vritra held up his hands. "Enough. Go get cleaned up.

You can speak to Miss Hunter in a couple of hours at supper."

The asura filed out, but Henna lingered.

"Did you want something?" Vritra asked her.

She looked to me, then back to Vritra. "Nah, I'll catch you later." She sauntered out.

"Well, that was … interesting."

He shrugged. "They're young and eager. The newest generation of asura. Not all of us slumbered; many opted to live in the mortal world and raise families. These are their children, more human than asura. This place is their home now, where they can learn about their heritage and their power. You're kind of a celebrity. The only asura in history, aside from me, who can shift into a dragon. So, be prepared for questions."

"So, they're all actually as young as they look?"

He nodded.

"Even Henna?"

"Henna was born on the celestial plains. She slumbered with rest of the gods, so she hasn't aged mentally or physically."

"The rest of the gods? Didn't you slumber?"

He offered me a crooked smile. “No.”

“So, what did you do? I mean, I didn’t know you existed until a few years ago.”

“I traveled.” He began dragging more mats together to make a larger sparring surface. “The mortal realm is filled with wonders, and I wished to see them all, from the pyramids to the hanging gardens. I lived in poverty, and I dined with kings. It was … educational.” He stood back to survey his handy work.

“So, what now?”

“Now we see how your dragon responds to threat. We put your power through its paces and give you the opportunity to connect and control it.”

“Okay. So, where is the threat?”

He gave me a shiver-worthy sadistic smile. “You’re looking at him.”

And then Vritra’s power slammed into me, knocking the breath from my lungs as it smashed right into my solar plexus. I doubled over, gasping for air. And he hit me again. What the fuck? The power inside me stirred, sitting up to take notice.

Defend dammit. Come on! Why was nothing happening?

“Come on, Miss Hunter. Defend yourself.”

“I’m trying.”

He slapped me with his aura—a taunting strike that had my hackles rising. Fuck this. Come on, dammit. Help me.

The dragon slid out of the box, testing the air. Power leaked out of me, rising off my skin. And when Vritra struck again, my power countered.

Yes!

Wait.

What was it doing? Not attacking but caressing … rubbing.

Vritra’s sharp intake of breath had my cheeks heating.

“No. Stop. Make it stop.”

Vritra tried to pull back, but the essence of my dragon wasn’t having any of it. She clung on, wrapping herself around his power, her sinuous body writhing against him. The shockwaves traveled back to wash over me, lighting up every nerve and synapse, sending messages of throbbing heat to my core. Oh, God. This was indecent and blatant and … so fucking good.

Vritra groaned low in his chest. His gaze locked with mine, eyes dark with desire, and then he was striding toward me. Running would be wise. Running was a good plan, but it wasn't what my body wanted. It needed to touch him and have him touch me, not just with his power but with his hands and mouth and tongue. His huge frame cast me in shadow, and then his hand twined in my hair, fisting it and yanking my head back. He claimed my mouth, desperate and out of control—teeth clashing, tongue on tongue desperate. We went down, slamming into the mats. Yes, yes. I wanted this, needed this. To feel him between my thighs, hard and ready and oh, fuck yes, move like that. Dammit, too many clothes in between the hardness and the wetness. The taste of his skin—sweet, fresh, cinnamon—it wasn't enough, not near enough. Not until he was inside me—deep inside. Rough calloused hands skated up my shirt. My hand slid down his pants to find his silken, huge, hardness.

"Carmella," he moaned into my mouth.

My groin throbbed, and heat pooled at my crotch. This dangerous, dynamic man was in my power. Mine …

"Ahem!"

The power, twisting and writhing above us, froze. Hearts beating rapidly, we stared into each other's eyes. Shock, awe, and longing swept across his face. Vritra pressed his forehead to mine, and then hauled his massive body off me.

Henna stood, arms crossed, brow arched. "Well, this is a new kind of training."

My power seeped back into me, settling back to sleep, done playing. I rolled to my feet and patted down my hair. The taste of him was in my mouth, his scent in my nose. Our power was no longer active, and yet my blood was still galloping through my veins.

Vritra stood with his back to me, hands on hips. His shoulders rose and fell erratically.

"Maybe Miss Hunter needs a slightly more impartial trainer," Henna suggested.

"Take her to supper and then see her out." Vritra's voice was hoarse and unsteady. He didn't turn to look at me, but strode from the room, slamming the door behind him.

Well, that was nice.

Henna snorted. “Oh, don’t look so dejected. It’s a compliment that he left. It means he wants you real bad, but respects you enough not to fuck you right here. Although, if I hadn’t come in, I’m sure you’d have coerced him into it.”

“What are you talking about?”

“Your hand down my father’s pants.” She shrugged. “Not really what a girl wants to see but …”

How the heck had we gone from sparring to … *that*? “Yeah, *that*. Totally not planned and super impulsive. I don’t know what happened. We were sparring and then my power … it went all weird.”

She smiled, and, for the first time since I’d met her, there was no malice in her expression. “Your dragon feels safe with my father’s. She knows he means her no harm, and so, sparring with him is pointless. If you want to master your power, you need someone your dragon doesn’t trust.”

“Like you?”

This time her smile was decidedly wicked. “Yeah, like me. So, what do you say? Wanna go a few rounds?”

She stepped onto the mats and began to circle me.

The dragon inside stirred. “Why not. Looks like my dragon isn’t averse to kicking your arse.”

She hit me, not with her asura power, but with her hand. It smashed into the side of my face and sent me flying. Oh, wow. That fucking hurt. Molten rage shot through my limbs, the pain vanished, and my dragon exploded out of its box, sending a wave of heat shooting toward Henna.

Henna leaped out the way, rolling and coming to her feet. “That’s more like it. Again.”

She attacked and my dragon answered.

I GAVE MY busted lip a final dab and winced as it tingled and healed up. Damn Henna and her cat like reflexes. The punch had rocked my world, and not in a nice way. The training mat was speckled with my blood. My lip had obviously been going for some kind of world record in bleeding out.

"So, your dragon is intuitive to your needs? She acts on your behalf?" Henna asked.

We were sitting on the benches at the back of the room, hydrating with bottles of water taken from the ice bucket behind us. Henna was fast and powerful, but my dragon was better. After the first violent attack, my power had realized that, although not a real threat, Henna was still willing to hurt me. And after being knocked off her feet for the fifth time, and managing to get in a sharp jab to my face, Henna had called time.

I swigged. "Yeah, it's weird, because with the armor skin my dragon knew I wasn't ready to let it go even before I did."

"So, you are connected, but not on a conscious level."

"I'm worried we may never be. She was cut off for so long. Maybe this is how it will be from now on."

"Is that so bad?"

I shrugged. "I don't know."

Henna played with the lid of her water bottle. "Do you have feelings for my dad?"

Oh … wow. How could I tell her that her dad was a suspect in my attempted murder? How could I, when my gut was telling me it couldn't possibly be true? If he wanted me dead, why train me? If he wanted me dead, why would my dragon trust him?

"So many feelings, but probably not the ones you mean."

"You looked like you were enjoying his attentions."

I blew out a breath. "I'm not always myself when I'm around your father."

"Maybe it's not you. Maybe it's your dragon that has the feelings."

My dragon … It made sense. My dragon power hadn't wanted to fight him. Instead, she'd wanted to … "Oh, man." I buried my head in my hands.

Henna chuckled. "Come on, let's get you some food. The other asura are dying to cross examine you about your power. For most of us, strength and agility is all we get."

"So, you don't have the kernel inside you?"

"Kernel?" Her brow crinkled. "Oh, you mean the reservoir?"

"Is that what it feels like for you? Maybe it's different for everyone."

She smiled wryly. "No, Carmella. It's different for you, because of who you are and what you are." She sighed. "As much as I hate to admit it, you're special."

"So … you don't want to kill me any longer?"

She let out a bark of laughter. "No. Not any longer." She screwed the lid back onto her bottle and stood.

"Henna, why did you try to kill me?"

She closed her eyes and shook her head. "It's a long, sorry tale. Not one for tonight, but maybe I'll tell you some day." She turned her head, and her lips curled in a sly smile. "Or maybe I'll change my mind and kill you just for fun." She jumped up and headed for the door. "Come on, the family is waiting."

Yeah, I preferred her when she'd been all malice. This sweet, sharing version of Henna was just creepy. Downing my water, I capped the bottle and followed.

Time to meet the rest of the family.

11

We took the lift down a floor.

"The young asuras' pad," Henna explained as we strolled down a corridor past several doors. "Suites. We take care of our own. Vritra is compulsive about keeping the old ways. A time when asura trained and fought battles together. He's all about unity and family."

The corridor opened up into a complex—a huge sprawling design with cinema room, pool, and communal lounge. But it was the kitchen Henna led me to. A table large enough to seat at least twenty was surrounded by asura stuffing their faces from a buffet-style spread.

My entrance killed the buzz of conversation and attracted every eye.

Henna tutted. "Enough with the staring. She can shift into a dragon, get over it."

Kiran waved me over. "Come sit with me."

Hmmm. A bit difficult when there were no vacant seats on his side of the table. "Where? On your lap?"

The guy beside him choked on his food.

Kiran's handsome face split in a grin, and he casually pushed the choking guy off his seat. "There you go."

The guy on the floor jumped up, punched Kiran's shoulder, and reclaimed his spot.

Henna shook her head and glanced at me. "Children, the lot of them."

"Hey, you're the same age as us!" a female asura with a cute bob said.

Henna's lip curled. "No, Gita. I'm not. We age differently on the celestial plains. In celestial years, I'm fucking ancient. Not to mention hotter than the lot of you put together."

Gita made a gagging nose.

"Ancient Henna with a stick up her arse," the guy seated in front of us muttered.

Henna's hand whipped out to smack him upside the head.

His drink sloshed everywhere and laughter rippled across the table.

Gita gave Henna a mock bow. "Thank you ancient one for deigning to hang out with us, not like the other ancients up at the top of the building who think we're tainted."

Kiran puffed out his chest and put on a booming voice. "Do better, Kiran. Make me proud, Kiran."

"Why are you crying, Kiran?" Henna mimicked the booming voice Kiran was putting on. "Stop getting your arse kicked by a girl, Kiran."

The group hooted with laughter. A chuckle rose up my throat. Yeah, I could get used to these guys.

My stomach grumbled. Urgh, what was wrong with me? So fucking hungry.

Henna pulled out a couple of seats this side of the table, and we parked our butts. A plate appeared before me, piled high with a little of everything. Thank the gods. It all smelled so good. I dug in. Yum, it was all delish. Wait, why had the room gone silent? I raised my gaze from my plate, mouth full of chicken.

Kiran was staring at me. In fact, they were all staring at me.

A quick glance down revealed why. I was a mess. Like food everywhere. I chewed and swallowed. “Sorry, just really hungry.”

The girl with the bob smiled. “No, it’s cool. It’s just, we’ve never seen anyone aside from Vritra eat like that.”

Yeah, there was food down my shirt and around my mouth. Henna passed me a napkin. What the heck was wrong with me?

“I don’t usually try to inhale my food.”

Henna snorted. “It’s a dragon thing. You just used a huge amount of power exercising her. She wants to be fed, and she doesn’t give a shit about etiquette.”

“Oh, my God!” Kiran said. “Can you imagine Vritra and Carmella having dinner together?”

Gita snorted.

The door opened and a hush fell over the gathered as Shukra strode in. Kiran ducked his head.

The sage strode over to the double ovens at the back of the kitchen and grabbed a plate. He ladled food straight from the pans onto his plate and then wandered over.

His gaze swept over us and snagged on me. "Miss Hunter, what a pleasant surprise," he boomed. "I'm glad you reconsidered your position and joined the fold."

"I haven't joined anything. I'm here to train."

His brows shot up. "Ah, the dragon inside. Powerful. Very powerful. And how was your training? No visible injuries? Good, very good."

I reached up to touch my lip, all healed now. "The advantages of super healing, I guess. A busted lip doesn't last long, although the mats may need a little cleaning."

Henna snorted. "She's a bleeder, this one."

Shukra made the appropriate concerned face. "Well, enjoy the food." He glanced at the table, and his eyes lit up. "Samosas." He reached across the table to the plate piled with the tiny triangular pockets of meat and vegetables. His sleeve trailed in the lentil soup. Tutting in annoyance, he pushed the fabric up his arm and out of harm's way, flashing the intricate tattoos decorating his skin: a crescent moon, a star, and the number eight.

My scalp prickled. There was something about that tattoo.

Shukra grabbed a handful of samosas. "I am sure we'll be crossing paths again soon, Miss Hunter." He popped the food onto his plate and left the room.

Kiran sagged, and Gita reached across the table to pat his hand. What the heck was going on?

Henna leaned in. "Shukra is Kiran's father."

"I thought Shukra was a sage, not an asura."

"He is," Kiran said. "My mum's an asura. They're not together anymore. Mum lives here on the uppermost floors, and dad, well, he likes his privacy."

"He has his own place in Camden," Henna said.

Well, that explained the booming voice Kiran had put on earlier. Wow, Shukra sounded like a bit of a dick.

"Well, the food won't eat itself," Gita said.

And just like that, all eyes were back on me. Fuck it, I was hungry and there was still food on my plate so … I picked up another drumstick and took a huge, indelicate bite.

Henna chuckled. “Yeah, Hunter, I think you’re gonna fit in just fine.”

The conversation turned to training, an upcoming tournament, and a grand prize. Such a huge difference from the pomp and ceremony of the covens. Maybe being an asura wouldn’t be so bad.

SHAITAN ENTERPRISES WAS a twenty-four-seven business. But the night receptionist was a far cry from Fanny. A monolith of a man seated in a wingback, a bucket of chicken at his elbow and a portable DVD player set up in front of him playing some romantic comedy.

I strode past, using my newly created access card to beep out of the barrier.

He hit pause and glanced up with a grin. “Hunter, right?”

"Yeah. And you are?"

"Rajan. Did you have fun with the gang?"

The gang? As in the asura? "You're an asura too?"

He inclined his head on his thick neck. "That I am."

"I didn't see you in the training room."

He wrinkled his nose. "Nah, don't go in for all the unnecessary violence. Not my thing."

No, romantic comedies seemed to be more his cup of tea. I wandered over and craned my neck to study the screen. "What you watching?"

"Serendipity. Have you seen it?"

"Yeah, good movie."

He nodded. "It is. The others would probably make fun of me if they weren't afraid I'd crush them."

"I thought you didn't do violence."

He grinned, showcasing huge, blunt teeth. "I said I didn't do *unnecessary* violence." He leaned down, opened a drawer, and retrieved something. "These are for you." He held out a key on a chain and a key card.

"What are they for?"

"Key's for the car parked outside, and the key card is to your penthouse suite on the uppermost floor."

A suite? What the heck was Vritra playing at? And why was I getting the warm fuzzies? "Um, thanks, but I have a flat."

He shrugged. "Hey, I'm just the delivery guy."

It was an invitation to reconsider my stance on the whole, I'm-not-running-away-from-possible-danger. My dragon was strong, and she liked me. She'd protect me. And if I got into deeper shit, then I had Paimon as back up. Giving up my life was a last resort. I dropped the keys and the card on the desk.

"Well, tell Mr. Ajagar that you delivered, and I politely declined."

He made an O with this mouth. "All the makings of a rom-com right here."

"Trust me. There is nothing romantic about any of this." I backed up. "See you around, Rajan."

And then I was out the door. The night was fresh and the breeze cool on my skin. My phone buzzed, and I answered without checking the ID.

Sobs filtered down the phone into my ear.

I gripped the phone tighter. “Hello? Hello? Who is this?”

“Oh, God. I can’t. I don’t understand.” It was Urvashi.

“Urvashi, calm down. What’s happened? Just calm down and talk to me.”

“I remember. I remember everything.”

12

Melody put her office phone back into its cradle. “Three more apsaras have suddenly got their memories back. The calls came in within minutes of each other. We have operatives bringing them in for questioning.”

Outside her window, London at night spread its wings. Every monument and landmark lit up blue, orange, or green.

Urvashi paced the office. “I need to know who did this. Who fucked with my head? Who killed … Oh, God. Why didn’t you tell me he was dead?”

She was talking about Devin, her Ghandarva lover. “I’m sorry.”

She shook her head. “It doesn’t matter. I’d forgotten we’d been together that night. I’d forgotten him.” She blew out her cheeks, grabbing hold of the edge of Melody’s desk to steady herself. “I feel sick.”

“Just sit, babe. Sit and we can go through it together.”

She nodded and parked her butt on one of the two padded seats on offer.

Melody perched on the edge of desk. “Any information, any details you can recall could be the key to catching these creatures.”

Urvashi licked her lips. “I remember Devin and I were just about to have sex. I was happy. We’d been seeing each other on and off for years, never getting serious but … he told me that night that he wanted to make it official. He wanted us to be an item. And then …” Her brow crinkled. “There was a crash … glass all over the place, and this black vibrating mass moving toward us. Devin tried to fight it. There was blood, and then another one came in through the busted window. It went for me, and then I … I think I blacked out.”

"Do you remember what happened to you afterwards?" Melody asked.

She shook her head. "No … No wait, there was a voice. I …" She winced, trying to summon the memory. "I knew who that voice belonged to, but I can't remember now. And then I was waking up in bed with a whole set of new memories."

Melody ran a hand over her face. "Okay, so we know that someone you knew was involved. What we don't know is how Devin got away. If whoever is behind this was willing to wipe Urvashi's memory to hide his or her scheme, then why let Devin go so easily?"

"Devin was one of the most powerful of the thirteen," Urvashi said. "Taking him down wouldn't have been easy. It's completely plausible that he escaped."

Escaped and made it back to his brothers, only to die days later. Even if we had succeeded in questioning him, he probably wouldn't have been able to identify his attacker. No one else could. Had we awoken him for nothing? Vritra claimed he probably would have died regardless, but we didn't know that, not for sure. Guilt clawed at my insides. The possibility that these creatures weren't from our world was becoming more and more plausible. Vritra and the witches at the Mayfair Ball had seen Paimon, but only the High Witch knew what he really was. It was time to bring Melody into the loop. The IEPEU needed to consider the possibility that more than one overlap may have occurred.

"There's something I need to tell you." I filled her in on the cuff, the djinn disappearances, the djinn realm overlapping with ours, and Paimon's desire to find the creatures. Yeah, a lot of filling in, a lot of stuff I probably should have told her days ago.

Melody paced the room. "You should have told us this sooner. Damn it, Hunter. Why didn't you pass on this vital information?"

"I don't know." There was no solid reason, just a conviction I'd had to keep the knowledge to myself. "At first it felt wrong to betray Paimon. He didn't want the overlap to be common knowledge. And then with the Kubera-style tech in the lab, and the fact that the creatures we're hunting knew about the Soho facility … it didn't make sense for them to be from another world."

"It still doesn't," Urvashi said. "I know that whoever is behind this is someone we know. I can't remember who was speaking, but I remember the words. He said, *don't fight it.* Those words and his voice are clear in my mind, like an aural photograph. If I heard that voice again, I'd be able to identify him."

Melody moved to the door and held it open. "Go home, get some sleep, and leave the rest to me. If you remember anything else, you let me know."

Urvashi nodded. "Of course."

"Hunter, if you're serious about being an operative with the IEPEU, then you cannot withhold information pertaining to a case."

She was annoyed with me, and it grated because she was right. I'd let my feelings for Paimon interfere with the case. The binding, the emotions, it had all been too much, and in the end, it had been a lie, because he hadn't come to me since the attack at the Mayfair Mansion. The connection between us was an illusion forged by the binding, nothing more. I'd compromised the case for smoke and shadow.

And there was the guilt again. "It won't happen again."

"Good. Murdoch's lined up the alpha interrogations for tomorrow, so make sure you're here, bright and early."

There was nothing I could do about the past. I'd fucked up. No changing that. But there was no way I'd be messing up these interrogations. I'd made Honey a promise I'd find the bastard who'd ordered the hit and make him pay.

I would not be breaking that promise.

THANK GOD THE day was over. The Yaksha interviews were a bust. If we could arrest them all just for being self-obsessed arseholes then we'd have a case. Rohan and Marco, my prime suspects, were open about wanting to control the Renegade Pack, and although this was possible motive for killing the Renegade Pack Alpha, it wasn't strong enough motive for killing them all. Honey's theory was sound, but upon examination it was clear that the death of so many yaksha was a negative impact on all the packs. If this was about setting up new treaties and readjusting boundaries, then whoever was responsible was doing a shoddy job, because as far as we could see, all that the new alphas had done was reaffirm the existing set-up.

Between catering to the hungry and pondering what our next move would be, my shift at the soup kitchen flew by and before we knew it, it was time to lock up and pack up. The night residents made their way up the stairs to the first floor and to bed.

Victor switched off the soup kitchen lights. "I'm walking you to aerial station. No arguments."

It was late, almost eleven. And the last tram left in twenty minutes. Tuesday nights were always super busy for some reason. "Look, I'll be fine. It's just around the corner."

He huffed and urged me out the door, locking up behind him.

"What about the residents?"

"The residents don't have Yamduth gunning for them."

He began to stride toward the station. "Come on."

Gah, there was no arguing with the rakshasa. "So, how are your friends?"

"Good."

"Are you planning on seeing them anytime soon?"

"Carmella, we don't have to make small talk."

"Oh. Good."

The steps to the station loomed up ahead. "I'll be okay from here."

"And I'll feel better once I see you safely on that tram."

"Such a gentleman."

Something dark flitted across his face but was gone too soon to decipher. The platform was empty, just the breeze and a lonely piece of litter rolling across the ground.

Four minutes till the tram arrived.

The thud of boots on the steps had Victor going into tense high alert mode.

"Chill, it's a tram station, people use it."

A head came into view, then another and another. Familiar faces, with familiar grins.

Henna, Gita, and Kiran strode toward us.

A surprised laugh escaped my lips. "What are you doing here?"

Henna shrugged, all nonchalant. "We were talking about you, and I mentioned the soup kitchen, so Kiran and Gita insisted on coming down to see it. I guess we left it too late."

Victor studied them silently.

"Hey?" Henna raised a hand in greeting. "I'm Henna."

"I know who you are. You tried to kill Carmella."

Gita gasped and Kiran choked on his own saliva.

Henna merely shrugged. "Yeah, but I've changed my mind, so …"

"You changed your mind? How magnanimous of you."

Henna cocked her head. "A big guy using a big word. I like it."

"We have a car," Kiran said. "We can give you a ride home."

"Thanks." We began walking back toward the steps.

"Parked up outside the kitchen actually," Kiran said.

The tram cables began to hum. A blast of hot air hit us in the face as several figures materialized between us and the stone steps.

Yamduth. Six, no seven of them, except they weren't toting the silver weapons today. These weapons were stark white. My gut twisted in warning. And Vritra's words came back to haunt me. New weapons. Weapons that could hurt me.

"Fucking hell." Henna pulled out a dagger.

The tram came roaring into the station.

"No!" I grabbed her arm and yanked her toward the slowing tram. "We need to board. Now."

Victor hesitated. Fuck the no contact rule. I grabbed his hand, tugging him along. The tram slid to a halt and we bundled on. The Yamduth were almost on us. Come on, come on, shut damn you. The doors obliged, and the tram shuddered into motion just as one of the yamduth slammed the flat of his hand against the glass.

He was smiling.

Why was he smiling?

"Fucking hell." Gita fell into the nearest seat. "Never thought I'd see a reaper and live to tell the tale."

A young couple who'd been tongue deep in each other's mouths surfaced for a second to see what all the commotion was about, and then resumed their mutual tonsil tickling.

A warm gust of air blasted through the tram. No. No, no, no.

Henna had a gaze fixed over my shoulder. "I think it may be time for some stabby, stabby after all."

Shit. I turned to face the reapers. Seven shadow-wreathed bringers of death in a tiny tram car built to carry twenty passengers at a push. The cars behind and in front were empty. Just us, the reapers, and the now frozen-with-fear lovers trapped behind the killers.

Kiran cracked his neck. "Bring it, bitches."

"Bring it, bitches?" Gita taunted. "That's the best you can do?"

The Yamduth began striding down the car toward us.

"Yeah?" Kiran said. "Let's see you do better."

"Reap this, bitches."

"Okay, that's pretty good, a play on the whole reaper reap thing."

"Will you two just shut the fuck up?" Henna snapped. "Focus, damn it."

The reapers raised their bone white swords … Bone. Motherfucker, the weapons were made of—shit! I ducked, slamming into the side of the car and scrambling to the side to get out the way.

My dragon roared into action, fire racing over my skin, but the pain was good. It meant armor. It meant protection. The sword came at me again, smashing into the seat to my left.

Someone screamed—probably the lovers. I leaped up, spun, and rushed the yamduth. I grabbed his sword arm and pushed it back. My dragon strength surged through me, battling his, and then his shadows swallowed my face, choking me and burning my eyes.

Dammit. I fell back, rolling away just in time to avoid the business end of his bone sword.

Thunk, thunk, thunk. He followed me down the aisle, swinging, missing. Way too close. And then I hit a wall. No. Not a wall. Someone's back.

"Hunter, watch out!" Henna grabbed the back of my shirt and threw me straight at the motherfucking window. Face meet reinforced whatever the fuck it was. Behind me, my friends fought the reapers, charging them, knocking them back, and doing their best to keep them off my back. The next stop wasn't for another five minutes.

Five minutes to stay alive.

Five minutes to avoid the slice of bone, because it *would* slice. The quiver in my gut, the roiling in my belly, told me this was a killing weapon. They'd figured out a way.

The asuras and Victor formed a barrier in front of me, protecting me from the reapers. The asuras were strong, Victor was a tank, but so were the yamduth with their acidic mist and death-dealing experience. And we were sorely outnumbered.

Gita fell to the ground, her shirt blooming red. Kiran yelled, leaping across the seats to get to her.

She was hurt bad. Henna screamed, jumping back as a yamduth's sword sliced through her top. Blood spattered across the windows. Victor grappled with another yamduth to my left. But there were four more wanting to play.

Time to even out the odds. I gripped the cuff on my wrist. *Paimon. Come on, I need you. Like real bad.*

The four yamduth closed in, eyes glowing, swords raised, ready to strike as one.

My dragon roared, expanding, desperate to take the reins. The world grew crimson. No. Not here. If I lost it, I could hurt the others. There was nowhere for them to run in such a confined space.

The dragon faltered.

Anything but that.

It shifted gears, sending a pulse of energy tunneling out from my solar plexus. It expanded on exit, smashing into the reapers and sending them back a couple of steps. Not enough though. Not nearly enough. They came at me hard and fast. A primal roar shook the cab, and Victor leaped over them to stand between us.

His shoulders heaved. He charged the four Yamduth. They met him head on, slamming into him, lifting him and hurling his body to the right. His huge frame smashed into the wall too hard, the whole car swung from side to side. He slid to the ground.

Slender arms wrapped around the yamduth leading the pack. Henna? Kiran attacked to my left, but it wasn't enough.

Paimon …

I sagged against the window, legs shaking. My dragon was spent. The blast of power she'd expelled had done us in.

Paimon wasn't coming …

I was done for. But no way was I going down without a fight. Come on legs. Stand the fuck up. Yes. I lifted my chin and stared those fuckers right in the eyes.

"Do it."

The center one stepped forward. "The bounty is at hand." He raised his sword.

"Fuck you."

A vibrating mass of darkness attacked the Yamduths from the left, sweeping them away from me and crushing them against the back of the tram.

Oh, God. Oh, fucking God. It was the creature—the one who'd tried to kill me, the one who'd taken me apart in the abandoned Guild facility under Soho.

Where the fuck had it come from? The tram was slowing down. The mass was whirring around the Yamduth—vibrating darkness against swirling shadows. And then the mass was flying backward, slamming against the same wall that Victor had hit a moment ago … that Victor had …

Oh, shit, it couldn't be …

The vibrating mass stopped moving, the darkness cleared.

Victor's unconscious form was revealed.

13

Victor was the creature.

No.

Please, no.

The air before me shimmered. “Seriously. You should do your own damned dirty work … Oh …” Amon turned to face me. “What in the world? Carmella is that you?”

Paimon had sent Amon. But crap, I had my armor on, and he didn’t recognize me, and there was no time. “It’s me, and those seven dudes are the bad guys trying to stab me with their bone swords.”

His eyes narrowed. “Well, we can’t have that.”

Henna and Kiran charged the Yamduth again, both bloody and battered, but Amon cut them off, striding up to the seven reapers, his body catching fire as he went.

The Yamduth, to give them credit, didn't falter. Amon whooped and flames *whooshed* toward the reapers, encasing them in a fiery halo. They continued to advance through the flames for a moment and then stopped.

The fire winked out and Amon crossed his arms. "Well, looks like you guys lost your boners."

The Yamduth stared at their empty hands. They traded glances, and then they did their favorite shadow-swirl disappearing trick.

"How?" Henna asked Amon. "How did you do that?"

Amon dusted off his hands. "Efreet fire burns through anything. Except, it seems, those creatures. They weren't too confident without their weapons though. No need to thank me. That was surprisingly satisfying. Any other beasts we need to vanquish?"

I glanced past him to the unconscious figure of my friend.

Henna followed my gaze. "I'm sorry, Hunter."

"Yeah. So am I."

THE IEPEU DARK cell unit was buzzing with the news of Victor's capture—a possible break in the case. Amon had winked out before the IEPEU arrived at the scene. There'd been no time to thank him for his aid or find out why Paimon hadn't come.

Victor was visible through the extra-thick, double-reinforced, one-way glass. He paced his cell like a caged animal—which he kinda was. The bars were thick and electrified. And runes were etched into every inch of the structure—the handiwork of the independent witches on the IEPEU payroll. The runes nullified power. So right now, Victor was perfectly harmless. But then, he hadn't fought or protested when they'd turned up to bring him in. And the compliance wasn't through fear they'd discharge their weapons. No. Bullets would do nothing to him if he went into vibrato mode. It was more than that. It was something in his eyes, something akin to relief.

"I need to see him. I have to speak to him." I headed to the door connecting our control room to the detainment chamber.

Parker sidestepped to block my path. "Not until Murdoch has finished with him. Look, I get that he's your friend. But going in there now could compromise the interrogation. You could unwittingly feed him information about the case that could—"

"He knows everything all ready. I told him what happened to me. There's nothing left to *feed* him. I can't believe he's responsible. There are other rakshasa out there. It doesn't have to be him. He's not the only one of his kind. This doesn't mean anything. I mean, he has two rakshasa friends for godsake." Excuses. My words sounded like desperate excuses, even to my ears.

Melody arched a brow. "He has two friends? The two guys that were at the soup kitchen when it was attacked by yaksha?"

"Yes."

Melody sighed. "You said there were three rakshasa at the lab that night."

Oh, shit. This looked bad. Bad for Victor. Bad for my conviction that he was innocent. "It has to be a coincidence."

Melody sighed. "Let Murdoch do his thing, meanwhile you need to give me the names of the other two rakshasa. We need to trace them and bring them in."

"I can't remember."

"Hunter …" There was warning in her tone.

She thought I was withholding information again "No. I mean it. I don't know their names."

Murdoch entered the room beyond the glass. He took a seat at the table facing the cage and switched on his tape recorder. Melody flipped a switch, and the speaker above us cracked with sound.

"Victor Reynolds, aged twenty-eight, arrested on charges of attempted homicide and several kidnappings."

Victor stopped pacing and faced Murdoch. "I didn't hurt anyone."

"Can you account for your whereabouts on the night of July the fifteenth this year?"

His brow crinkled. "I was at the soup kitchen. I'm always there in the evening."

Murdoch glanced at the glass and Melody nodded. She flipped through a file in front of her. "Hunter, the night you were attacked, you said you visited the soup kitchen. Was Victor there?"

Honey had been there helping Mira, who'd been in her adult Caro skin. I'd asked where Victor was and they'd shrugged. Oh, God.

"Hunter?"

I swallowed. "No. I didn't see him there."

Melody slipped on an earpiece. "He wasn't at the kitchen that evening, Murdoch."

Murdoch didn't give any indication that he'd heard her, but his next words told us he had. "In that case, you'll be aware that Miss Hunter paid the kitchen a visit that night, before she was attacked. She claims you weren't on the premises."

Victor began to pace again. "I was. I'm always there."

"Maybe Miss Hunter is lying then?"

"No, Carmella wouldn't lie. And that night isn't something she'd forget." He pinched the bridge of his nose.

"Do you wish to change your statement? Let me ask again. Were you at the soup kitchen on the night of the fifteenth of July?"

"I … I can't remember."

"You can't remember. All right." He rattled off a bunch of dates, and I recognized one—the date Urvashi had gone missing. "Where were you on these dates? Can you confirm your whereabouts on *any* of those dates?"

Victor ran his hands over his head. "I need my diary."

"Your diary?"

"Yes, it has a list of the missing times."

"I'm sorry, Mr. Reynolds. I don't understand."

Victor sighed. "The blackouts. I made a note of all the times when I … lost time."

"How convenient," Murdoch drawled. "You keep a list of the times you kidnapped an apsara, and make a note of your almost homicide, and then claim theses entries represent time lost?"

Victor's chest heaved. "It's the truth. If I did do those things, I don't remember."

Murdoch nodded. "Fine, we'll retrieve your diary, but let me ask you this: did Miss Hunter tell you about her attack?"

Victor's mouth turned down. "Yes."

"Did she describe her attackers to you?"

Victor squeezed his eyes shut and nodded.

"And so, you knew exactly what creatures had attacked her."

Victor exhaled. "I suspected. Yes."

"And yet you kept this information to yourself. Why?"

"Because rakshasa aren't killers. Despite what you may believe, violence isn't our way. If we do fight, it's for survival. There aren't many of us left, and I know the ones that exist. None of them would do such a thing. I believed that what attacked Carmella was something new, something similar yet different."

"Let's say I believe you. Assume that everything you've just told me is true. Why didn't you make the connection between your missing time and Miss

Hunters attack? Didn't you wonder if maybe the culprit *could* be you, and that maybe you just didn't recall?"

Victor groaned, burying his face in his hands. "Yes, of course I did. You have no idea how much it's tormented me, but I care about Carmella. I would never hurt her. Even if I wasn't in control of my mind, even if someone was making me do these things, my instincts would be to protect her."

"Melody." I grabbed her arm. "Oh, God. I think it *was* him. He attacked me at my flat, but instead of killing me, he knocked me out and hid me in the apartments under Soho. I think he was trying to keep me away from the other two rakshasas. And at the end, only two creatures attacked me. He didn't participate." The fact that they kept their other form a secret hadn't helped us identify them. If the yamduth hadn't attacked me, then he wouldn't have had to reveal his hidden form. "Plus, he revealed himself to save me from the Yamduth."

Melody sighed. "Yeah, he did." She switched on the mike on her headset. "Murdoch, take a break. We need to talk."

The temperature dropped, and an all too familiar cool breeze blew across my skin. Melody glanced up at the air vent in the wall.

It wasn't the AC acting up. This was something else. It had my pulse racing and my stomach fluttering. Breathe, Carmella. Just act casual.

He materialized in front of me, and Melody had her gun pointed at him before either of us could breathe.

"Don't move," she said.

Paimon ignored her, his gaze fixed on me. "Where is it?"

"Hunter? You know this guy?" Melody asked.

"It's Paimon."

"The djinn?"

"Yeah." I couldn't take my eyes off him: his eyes, his nose, his mouth, you know, all the little things making up the face that haunted my dreams. The jump in my pulse, and the skip in my heartbeat were proof—this was more than the after-effects of the binding. Was he feeling the same? Hard to tell when he was glaring at me as if I'd kicked his puppy.

"Carmella, where is the creature?" he asked.

"Amon told you?"

"Of course he told me. And it's lucky he did, because it seemed like you had no intention of calling me."

"I did call you, remember? But you sent your brother."

Melody cleared her throat and lowered her weapon. "Someone care to fill me in on what the fuck is going on? How did you get into the complex? This area is for authorized personnel only."

He kept his attention on me, but addressed her question, his jaw tight. "Your security means little for those of us who travel the in-between."

His tone, his attitude, everything grated. My dragon stirred, affronted on my behalf.

Paimon's gaze narrowed. "When were you going to call me?"

I stood up straighter. "When I was fucking ready."

He flinched. "You have the creature in your custody, yes?"

"Yes." My gaze slipped past him to the reinforced glass through which Victor was clearly visible, pacing in his cage.

"Then the deal is done. Give him to me. We will mete out justice in my realm."

"Whoa!" Melody held up her hands. "No one is taking anyone anywhere."

The door opened and Murdoch entered. His gun was in his hand so quickly it looked like it had just materialized out of thin air. How the fuck did they draw weapons so fast?

"Parker? Do we have a situation?" Murdoch asked.

"It's all right, Murdoch. He's one of the *good* guys," Melody replied.

Yeah, he was supposed to be, but right now I wasn't so sure. "I don't know how things work in your realm but in mine, you're innocent until proven guilty."

Paimon exhaled through his nose. "So he *isn't* the same creature that took my people."

"At this point, we believe he was involved, but he doesn't recall any of it. We believe he was somehow controlled or brainwashed."

"You *believe*? But do you have any solid proof?"

"Not yet, but—"

He held up his hand, and I almost lost my shit. The dragon surged upward in indignation, burning a path up my throat.

"He has taken djinn," Paimon said. "And we have a right to know what he has done with them."

Was he not listening to me? "But he doesn't remember anything."

Paimon closed his eyes, chest rising and falling. "The absence of memory does not absolve him of the crime. If what you say is true, then my people may never know the fate of their loved ones. The ascendant djinn who were taken may be lost to us forever. The creature who took them from us must pay the price."

"No. There is someone else involved. Someone pulling the strings. *That's* the person you want."

His expression softened slightly. "Do you have this person?"

"No. Not yet but—"

"In that case, you have the only person I need. Justice must be served."

Murdoch holstered his gun. "Is this the djinn you briefed us on Parker?" He fixed a reproving glare on me. "The one Hunter failed to mention when debriefed after her attack."

Melody nodded absently and took a step toward Paimon. "Look," she said sympathetically. "I understand you want justice. But lynching a man just because he's the only one you can get your hands on *isn't* justice. We need to work on getting to the root of the problem."

Paimon's lips tightened. "We don't have the time. My people are filled with a rage you are incapable of comprehending. There is talk of invasion, of war; and trust me, you do not want war with the djinn. Our worlds may have overlapped, but you do not want the djinn invading your homes and your lives. Not all of us are as … sympathetic to humanity as I."

This was bad, and the pallor of Melody's skin told me she agreed. We'd not long ago avoided being annihilated by the void. Another war could be the end of us. The djinn were a different breed. They did magick without a skein, and could move between time and space. If they attacked, we were fucked. But there was no way I was throwing Victor under the bus.

I lifted my chin. "I won't let you take him."

Paimon's nostrils flared. "You cannot stop me."

Oh, man. Maybe if I appealed to his other side, the side that appreciated humanity? "Victor is a good man, a decent man. I know in my heart that none of this is his fault."

"Your heart cannot be entered as evidence."

"Enough." Melody stepped between us. "We *can* crack this case. We just need a little more time."

Paimon turned his attention to her. "You have two days. After that, we will come for him, and there will be nothing you can do to stop us."

He stepped back and vanished into thin air, leaving us gaping at an empty space.

"Well that was fun," Murdoch said. "On a separate note, I believe the rakshasa. I think he's someone's puppet."

"Good," Melody said. "Then we're on the same page."

The intercom buzzed, and a harassed voice filled the room. "Um. Miss Parker? We have a situation at reception. Please come. Now."

Parker hit the button to speak direct to the receptionist. "What is it, Carly?"

"Ghandarva. And lots of them."

"What are they doing here?" And then it hit me. The rakshasa had killed one of their brothers.

"They're here for Victor."

14

Twelve winged, furious Adonises filled reception. Their wings were tucked away, invisible to our eyes but even without them on display, the Ghandarva were a force to be reckoned with, and we had something they wanted.

Murdoch had stayed behind to monitor Victor, but I'd insisted on coming down with Melody. They knew me. Maybe I could talk some sense into them?

Ajit and Rudi, the two Ghandarva who'd administered to their dying brother Dharma, stood ahead of the flock. Their attention locked on us as we approached. Melody stopped at the barrier.

"How can we help you?" she asked.

Ajit ignored her and fixed his gaze on me. “You have the creature who killed our brother. Give him to us.”

“I’m sorry, but we can’t do that.”

“You can, and you will. He has wronged us, and we will have justice.”

I was sick of this. First Paimon and now him. “Really? You think you’re the only one that he’s wronged? What about me? Those creatures killed me. Tore me apart. Have you forgotten that?”

He blinked, taken aback.

“Oh, don’t give me that look. You found out we had the creature in custody so you obviously have contacts, there’s no way you didn’t know about the lab incident.”

He pressed his lips together. “So, you wish to keep him for yourself? To exact justice?”

“No. I wish to find out who the fuck is really behind all this shit. Victor is merely a puppet, and I want to find out who’s pulling the strings.”

Rudi leaned in to whisper something in Ajit’s ear, and Ajit nodded.

"You have two days to find the puppeteer. After that we will—"

"Do nothing," I interrupted, rage swelling in my chest as my dragon awoke. "You will let the IEPEU do their job, and you will back the fuck off!"

Ajit's face contorted with fury, but I was done giving a shit.

"If you want justice, get off your feathered arses and help us search for the person responsible, don't just swan down here after we've done all the work and expect privileges. You want to live in this world, then you better damn follow the rules. Your wings and your fancy tower meant jack shit to this killer. So, maybe you need to reassess how much power you actually have."

The tension in the room had just ratcheted up a notch. Ajit took a step toward the barrier, and I caught movement in my periphery. The Ghandarva paused, his gaze slipping over my head, and then he stepped back.

"Keep us informed on what you find," he said.

I kept my gaze on him, even though the urge to glance over my shoulder was a burning pain between my shoulder blades.

"Now if that's all, we have an investigation to get back to," Melody said.

Ajit nodded curtly, and, behind him, Rudi's eyes flashed dangerously. But they left, striding out into the street. Cries of awe filtered in through the partially open entrance as the flock took to the skies.

The adrenaline rush abated, and my knees buckled. I made a grab for the barrier to steady myself. Had I just done that?

"You did great," Melody said.

I turned to see what had given Ajit pause, and a strange warmth infused my limbs at the sight of the IEPEU operatives behind me, weapons holstered but at the ready. They'd had my back, and for the first time since I'd started working here, I felt like I belonged.

ALTHOUGH I'D MANAGED to smack down the Ghandarva's ultimatum, Paimon's still stood.

Two days to find the real culprit behind the djinn disappearances, and all I could think about was the way Paimon *hadn't* looked at me. I was a desperate fool crushing on the unavailable guy. He'd sent Amon to save me and come only when he'd known we had Victor in custody.

Victor was lying on his back on the floor of his cage, eyes closed. Two days to save his life, like he'd tried to save mine. Could we do it? I'd shown my face, told him I believed him and was doing everything in my power to get him out of this mess, but he'd kept his head down, as if ashamed to look me in the eyes.

My heart ached for him.

My fists ached to pummel the fucker who'd done this to us.

Victor's friends were being questioned. So far, it was a similar tale about losing time. If they'd spoken to each other about their experiences they may have realized something dodgy was going on. Victor would have made the connection sooner. He would have come to me. But rakshasa were loners. These three were friends, but not the kind that shared their fears. And someone had used that to their advantage, banking on them not talking about the blackouts.

We were getting close, so close to finding out just who that person was, because right now, Melody was picking up the reports that may hand us the missing pieces of the puzzle.

She strode into the room, her eyes bright. "We got the results of the diagnostics the tech team ran on the machines. Those results, coupled with what we know about the apsaras' memory loss and the details in the manual we found in the lab, mean it's safe to conclude that the rakshasa were under the influence of the protsaahan taken from the apsara."

"So, someone used the apsaras' persuasion to control them? Wait. That doesn't make sense. The rakshasa kidnapped the apsara so the mastermind could extract the protsaahan. How would he have controlled them to do that?"

Melody riffled through a sheaf of papers and pulled out a statement. "This is the statement of the first apsara who went missing. Her account differs from the rest. She didn't describe a vibrating, black mass. She claims she was attacked by a masked figure." Melody laid the paper flat on the desk in front of me. "She drew this."

It was a symbol. Like an eight on its side. Something niggled at the back of my mind. "I've seen this before."

"It's the symbol for infinity."

"Yeah, but I …" An arm … I'd seen it on an arm. "Shukra. He has this symbol on his arm."

Melody went still. "He's also one of the three people who knew about the feather."

My heart was pounding. "It's not enough evidence though, is it?"

"No."

"We need Urvashi. We need her to hear his voice."

15

The bathroom lights flickered. I turned off the taps and stared at my reflection. The word exhausted came to mind. Tomorrow was a big day, and if we were wrong, then it would be the last time I'd see Victor and his friends alive, because Paimon would be as good as his word and take them from under our noses.

Parker and Murdoch had it all set up. A ploy to get Shukra into the building, to get him in a room with me under controlled conditions. Shukra was a sage, responsible for the emotional and spiritual wellbeing of the asuras. It was his duty to provide them with guidance and support in times of crisis. For the purpose of this entrapment, *I* was the asura in crisis—struggling with my identity—or so Parker had told him over the phone. It was, apparently, affecting my performance, and Shukra was coming into the office to speak to me tomorrow. Urvashi would be in the adjoining room, listening in, and as soon as she gave the word the IEPEU would move in. But if we were wrong, if we couldn't tie Shukra to the case with this final piece of evidence, then it was over. We'd be out of time.

Stripping down to my knickers, I pulled on my favorite bedtime T-shirt. The necklace Banner had gifted me got caught on my hair and I freed it, allowing it to settle back against my collar bone. I hadn't dare wear this T-shirt when bound to Paimon.

Paimon.

A breeze trickled in through the partially open window, got caught by the desk fan and blasted around the room. The cuff on my wrist winked at me tauntingly in the lamplight. Accepting it had saved my life, but now it was time to let him go. Now, how did this clasp work?

My fingers fumbled then froze as a shiver skipped up my spine and gooseflesh broke out up my thighs.

"Carmella?"

He was here, standing behind me, and my mouth was suddenly as arid as the bloody desert. Licking my lips and swallowing a couple of times to moisten my throat, I turned to face him.

His fancy clothes were gone. Instead, he was dressed in loose dark pants and an unbuttoned billowy cream shirt. It looked butter yellow in the light of the lamp.

I lifted my chin. "What are you doing here? Did you have more threats to make?"

"I'm sorry."

Okay, I hadn't been expecting that. "Look, I get that you're in an awkward position with your council wanting justice. I get you're trying to prevent a war. But your attitude sucked."

He took a step toward me, and the atoms in the air were suddenly charged with electricity.

"I'm not sorry about what I said, or about my attitude."

Huh?

"I'm sorry for not coming when you called."

Oh. The pulse at my throat skipped. "No big deal. You're not obligated. Mira explained that when she gave me the cuff." I took a deep breath. "In fact, I think you should have it back." I made to unclasp it.

He bridged the gap between us and wrapped his hand around my wrist, covering the cuff. "Please. Don't."

He was touching me and strange things were happening—unwanted fluttering and yearnings.

He moved closer, his cool breath fanning across my fevered brow. "I wanted to come. I wanted to." He pressed his forehead to mine and our breath mingled.

"Then why didn't you?"

He pulled back slightly, tipping my chin upward with the crook of his index finger to look down into my face. My lungs grew tight at the proximity, the otherworldness of him, the cosmic stars in his eyes as his gaze lingered on my lips. He bridged that gap too, stealing my breath with a brush of his lips, claiming my mouth with a sweep of his sweet tongue. I opened to him with a gasp, my body instantly on fire with need. His chest rumbled, and then his tight control snapped. His hands twined in my hair, and he deepened the kiss, branding me with tongue and teeth. We swayed, falling back onto the sofa-bed. His thighs slipped between mine, his torso covered me. His shirt, so soft yet unnecessary, fell prey to my eager hands. His skin beneath, like velvet silk, begged to be caressed and tasted. Peaches, he tasted like peaches. I was drowning in him, senses intoxicated, heart aching to burst from my chest with a tumult of emotions. His arousal rubbed up against my wet knickers, sending electric heat coursing through my veins. He pushed my shirt out of the way, fingers dancing across my hips and slipping into my knickers. Lean, long fingers. Almost there. Oh, please.

My dragon stirred in confusion, shaking herself awake to assess the situation. I wanted this man in ways I'd never wanted anyone before. I wanted him inside my body, inside my soul, but he belonged to another.

"Carmella …" Paimon raised his head, locking gazes with me. His voice was a tortured rasp of desperate desire.

I cupped his jaw, pressing kisses to his face. My eyes burned because, as much as we both wanted it, this couldn't happen. He wasn't mine to have.

He closed his eyes. "I wanted to be there, but I couldn't, because I was with Alara."

I'd known. Deep down, I'd known. Alara was his betrothed—the key to an important alliance.

He carefully pulled my shirt down to cover me and climbed off the bed. "Alara awoke, and I was duty-bound to tend to her. She remembered nothing of import though."

I swung my legs off the bed. "You need to stay away from me." It wasn't a demand, just a statement of fact.

"I know."

"This was wrong. So wrong." I pinched the bridge of my nose, anger flaring in my chest at the injustice of it all—at my stupidity in almost becoming the other woman. Unclasping the cuff, I slipped it off and held it out. "Please. Take it."

Paimon stared at the golden bracelet, his expression tortured. "Without it, I will not be able to find you so easily."

I swallowed the dastardly lump in my throat. "I know."

He didn't take it.

"You're marrying another woman, Paimon. I can't do this. I can't have you in my life if you can't be mine." There, I'd said it. The weight that should have lifted grew heavier, grabbing me by the throat and squeezing until tears leaked from the corners of my eyes. "Your heart can't be compromised either."

His nostrils flared. "It already is."

Fucking hell. He was going to break me. My vision blurred. "Please … take it and go. I can't …" A sob caught in my throat.

His mouth twisted in agony. "Don't. Please, I do not want to cause you pain."

"Then take the damn cuff."

He plucked it from my fingers and turned it over in his hands. "I had this specially crafted for you. Look at it, so tiny, so delicate, and yet forged of indestructible material. Just like you." His expression smoothed out. "There's something you need to know. It's the other reason I found you tonight."

Dread reared its head. "What is it?"

“Earlier, while I was with you, the council met again. It has been decided that only the head of the person responsible for the djinn abductions and concrete evidence of the fate of our missing djinn, or their safe return, will suffice.”

“Wait. What does that mean?”

“It means that if you cannot hand over the mastermind of the scheme and provide us with answers as to the fate of our missing djinn, then our armies will invade your world to eliminate any further possible threats to ours.” He delivered the lines dispassionately.

The ticking clock sped up. “I’ll let the IEPEU know. You should leave now.”

He inclined his head and took a step back, taking my heart with him. “Carmella, you should also know … if I were free to choose …” He vanished.

“Dammit, you’re not supposed to say shit like that!” I was crying openly now. My power bloomed, sending a comforting heat through me and rocking me in its armored embrace.

Stronger than this.

Harder than this.

Asura.

MY SLEEP WAS interrupted by a knock at the door. Tugging on a pair of leggings, I answered to the tummy-grumbling smell of my favorite kind of food.

Banner held the take-out bag of Chinese food up as an offering. “Can I come in?”

I stepped back to allow him to enter.

He popped the food on the kitchen counter and began rummaging for plates.

I sighed. “I’ll do it.”

“No. Just sit down and let me.”

I was too tired to argue with him, it was just kinda nice to have someone take care of me. A hard kick and firm shove had the bed folding back into its alternate personality—the sofa. The coffee table was shoved up against the wall, and it took less than a second to drag it forward.

Banner joined me with two plates piled high with food.

We ate in silence for about five minutes and after a while, even though the ache in my heart remained, the one in my stomach dissipated.

Banner set his plate on the table. “Why didn’t you call me?”

“What?”

“You were attacked at the aerial tram station.”

I dropped my fork onto my plate. “Things happened so fast afterward. I didn’t think. How did you find out?”

“The supernatural grapevine.”

No idea what that was, but hey. “I would have called you. It’s just things are delicate right now, there’s stuff that needs to be sorted, and we’re on a clock.” That damned lump was back in my throat. The one you get when you know you’ve failed, or lost something really important, and you know things will never be the same again. I fucking hated that lump.

“Carmella, talk to me.”

So I did. I told him about Paimon, about the overlap and the djinn. I told him about the binding and how it was all connected to the missing apsara and how we were finally on the cusp of catching our man.

His eyes darkened. “Who is it? Who’s the bastard behind this?”

I couldn’t give him our suspect’s identity, not without breaking protocol. “That’s classified. But I can tell you this: if he turns out to be the wrong guy, then we’re out of time. The djinn will attack our world as vengeance. They’ll annihilate us just to make sure we can never harm them again.”

Banner turned away, his face pale. “A war?”

I snorted. “You could call it that. But more likely it’ll be an extermination. The guy who organized the abductions of the ascendant djinn got lucky. He caught them one at a time, unawares. They couldn’t track the creature because the signature it left behind was too weak. And because every djinn taken was alone at the time of their abduction, there were no witnesses—no description of the attacker. The djinn didn’t understand our world, didn’t have the scent of all the creatures living in it. But now they do. They know what they’re hunting, and if they come, we don’t have a chance. They don’t need the skein to do magick. They can travel from one location to another in the blink of an eye. I think they may be more powerful than our gods."

"If they declare us hostile, then we're fucked," Banner surmised.

"Pretty much."

"Suddenly, I'm not that hungry anymore."

"Yeah, neither am I, but if this is gonna be one of my last days on earth, then I'm damned if I'm letting good food go to waste."

Banner watched me for a few beats and then picked up his fork. "You know, Carmella, every time I think I have you figured out, you just go and do an about-face on me."

He wasn't the only one trying to figure me out. I still had a long way to go, and all the crap that kept happening didn't leave me much time to do much figuring of anything. Hopefully, tomorrow would bring closure to the case, and it would be time for some introspection.

16

The room we'd chosen for the entrapment was on the fifth floor of the IEPEU. A windowless space used for training courses in administrative type stuff. A smart screen and rows of desks fitted with touch-screen monitors made up the interior. The lights were the horrible anemic kind. You'd think with the kind of funds this place had, they'd invest in better illumination.

Murdoch checked the audio connection cable hidden in the upper left-hand corner of the room.

"The lifts will be disabled upon Shukra's arrival," he said. "The emergency doors will be put into lockdown. Once he's in here with you, if he is our guy, there'll be no escape." Murdoch handed me a state-of-the-art earpiece. "Remember, we just need him talking for a few minutes. If you can get him to say the words the witness heard that would be great. Just relax, and let him lead the conversation."

"Let's just get this over with."

Murdoch left the room.

"Can you hear me, Hunter?" Parker's voice came in through the tiny mic nestled in my ear.

"Loud and clear."

"We just had another breakthrough. The tech department was examining the rakshasas' mobile devices, looking for clues, and they found something interesting."

"Go on."

"Some kind of code imbedded into their mobiles. It's unlike anything we've ever seen before, they're still analyzing it, but when it's activated a symbol comes up. Guess what it is?"

"The infinity sign."

"You got it."

"So we nail him with this and we got him for sure?"

"Damn straight." Her voice dropped. "Okay, he's just exiting the lift now. Murdoch has him and is leading him to the room. The line we need if possible is *don't fight it*. Look annoyed. You don't want to be here, remember?"

Frown in place, I turned as the door opened and rolled my eyes. "For godsake."

Shukra smiled warmly and closed the door behind him. "Miss Hunter. It's so good to see you again."

"Wish I could say the same."

He parked his butt on the edge of the nearest desk. "Come now, it's not so bad, is it? We're long overdue a chat. You know what I am?"

"A busy body who likes to dig around inside other people's heads?"

He let out a sharp bark of laughter. "Well, I can honestly say I've never been described like that before."

"Look, I don't need this. I don't need you, and I don't need to be an asura."

"You're doing great," Parker said into my ear.

Shukra made a sympathetic face. "Denying who you are isn't healthy. You're part of something bigger, united to a divine force that many would kill to join with."

I shook my head, attempting a conflicted expression. "I can't, it's just too much. It's suffocating."

"Don't fight it, Miss Hunter. The more you fight, the worse it will be."

He'd said the words. Had Urvashi heard them? Was it him?

"That's it. Positive ID," Parker said.

The door burst open, and Murdoch strode in flanked by IEPEU operatives, weapons at the ready.

"What is this?" Shukra was on his feet, looking from me to the officers.

"Shukra, you are under arrest for kidnapping and attempted murder, you—"

"No." He shook his head violently. "You have it wrong."

The operatives moved toward him.

Shukra rolled up his sleeve, and his tattoos came to life, writhing and glowing. He slammed his hand over the infinity symbol and vanished.

"What the fuck just happened?" Murdoch said.

"I think we just found out what that symbol can do."

DID THEY HAVE him? Why hadn't Parker called? Surely they'd have him by now.

Murdoch looked up from his desk. "Sit down, Hunter, before you wear a hole in the damned carpet."

I parked my butt behind my desk but was back on my feet in less than two seconds. "Why hasn't she called?"

Murdoch leaned back in his seat and surveyed me for a long beat. "It will be all right. They'll find him, and the djinn will get the answers they need, but …"

"What? But what? Gah, I hate it when people leave their sentences hanging like that."

"We're not in the habit of handing over our citizens to foreign worlds."

"Not in the habit? We've never been in this position before. He kidnapped djinn, he kidnapped apsara, and he tried to kill me. Who knows what he's done with the missing djinn. We refuse to hand him over and we're fucked."

Murdoch smiled wryly. "You underestimate our government, Hunter."

"Look, we can argue about this once we have the sage in custody." I glared at my mobile. "Ring, damn you."

"How's your friend? Urvashi, is it?"

"I sent her to the canteen for coffee. I'm not letting her out of the building until we have Shukra in custody. Flipping heck, with that symbol he could be bouncing around all over the place."

The phone rang. Thank god. "Parker? You got him?"

"No. He didn't go back to Shaitan Enterprises," Parker said.

"Fuck. Wait. He has a residence on the outskirts of Camden. Speak to Kiran, his son. He was there when I was attacked by Yamduth. He tried to save my life. Tell him the truth, and then call me back with the address."

"Why?"

"Because I'm coming with. If he's there, I'll hang back. If not, I can case the place for clues."

"We'll question Kiran, but this could get back to Vritra, and we haven't cleared him as an accessory yet."

"I trust him." The words popped out instinctively.

"You do?"

"He wouldn't hurt me. I know it."

She blew out a breath. "If you were anyone else, I'd tell you to take a leap. But I know you, Hunter. You have an uncanny instinct for people. I'll get the address. I just hope we're in time."

"Wait. Don't forget to call me."

"Copy that." She hung up.

"Better?" Murdoch said.

"Not until we have our guy."

He studied me. "You're hoping the Yamduth attacks are somehow linked to him too, aren't you?"

"No, I hadn't even thought of that, but yeah, that would be great." Kill two birds with one stone and all that. "I doubt it though. There's no motive. He sent the rakshasa after me because he wanted the feather, and he couldn't leave me alive to tattle about his messengers. But the feather is gone, and the IEPEU have detailed descriptions of the creatures, so I'm no longer a threat."

Murdoch pouted. "I just can't shake the feeling that there's more to this than we're being presented with."

The phone beeped with an address. I grabbed my bag. "You coming?"

He shook his head. "Nope, this one is all yours."

I headed out the door and down the stairwell, fuck waiting for a lift. I had a sage to catch.

I ARRIVED TO find the IEPEU unit already on the scene. Parker met me at the front door to the detached red-brick house.

"We were too late," she said.

"He got away?"

"No. He's dead."

"What?"

"Suicide. Slit wrists. He bled out."

No. That didn't make sense. "Why would he kill himself?"

Parker held up a clear plastic bag containing a note. "He left this."

I took it from her carefully and scanned the words—something about guilt and shame, honor and desperation, the need for power, to be divine. My stomach sank. He'd wanted to be a god and was trying to create his own amrit, the ambrosia of the gods. The main ingredient had been djinn souls. He went on to explain how he'd found out about the abandoned Soho guild operations. The equipment had been sourced from an old Kubera lab under Richmond Park. His first apsara abduction, the extraction of protsaahan and the selection of rakshasa to bring him what he needed. It was all explained. Victor had said he had contacts at Shaitan Enterprises; it turned out that rakshasa were also a kind of demigod. Shaitan Enterprises welcomed them, provided jobs and homes if they needed—so it had been easy for Shukra to find his victims, to use protsaahan to persuade them to do his bidding. The eternity symbol had been the trigger. It showed up on their phones, and they'd drop what they were doing and convene at the Soho lab for instruction. Another call, another flash of that symbol, and they'd snap out of it, until next time. He'd kept them topped up, forcing them to bring him enough apsara to extract enough persuasion to last weeks. Everything was in the note, but it felt all wrong.

"Parker! Down here!"

Parker jerked her head to indicate I follow. We walked through the kitchen to a door leading down into a basement. Urgh, this didn't look good. Flashlight beams bounced around at the bottom of the steps. Melody grabbed her pen light, leading the way.

"Bulb's busted," Drake, her second in command, called out.

We joined him at the foot of the steps.

"This way." He led us to the left, past shelves piled high with crap, to another door in the wall. The rest of her team was inside the brightly lit chamber beyond.

What the heck? It was a lab of some sort, but the two things that caught my attention were the huge furnace and the glowing orb suspended in a cradle on the lab counter. The inside swirled like a lava lamp, pulsing enticingly.

“What is it?” Parker asked.

Another operative was flicking through a notepad on the counter. “Djinn souls. He burned the bodies in the furnace. That’s all that’s left.”

“So, we have a dead sage, a confession, and all the evidence we need to tie this up in a big red bow and hand it over to your friend Paimon.”

“Yeah.” I drew out the syllable.

Parker locked gazes with me. “It feels almost too neat, doesn’t it?”

“Convenient. I mean, who stops to write an essay when they have the IEPEU on their tail?”

Drake joined us. “You think it’s a set up?”

“He said we had it wrong. Back at headquarters, when Murdoch barreled in, he said we had it wrong.” I walked over to the orb—the glowing sphere which contained the main ingredient to Shukra's homemade amrit. "Where are the notes on synthesizing the amrit?"

The operative studying the papers shook his head. "Nothing in here about amrit."

Made no sense, and there was something else niggling at me, an important clue staring me right in the face.

Boots clattered down the stairs.

"Hey, you can't be in here!" Drake said.

My dragon felt his presence a split second before he entered the room.

"Where is he? Where's Shukra?" Vritra demanded.

Parker stepped forward. "His body is upstairs in the master bedroom, you can't—"

But he was already off, back up the stairs to find his friend.

My heart lurched for him. Shukra had been his confidant. This had to hurt like a bitch.

I walked toward the stairs. "I best make sure he's okay."

Melody nodded.

I found Vritra in the bedroom doorway, his hand over his mouth as he stared at Shukra's dead body.

"I'm sorry." I reached for him.

"You should have come to me." His tone was brittle.

"What?"

He turned to me, his anger a primal, tangible force pressing against me. "You are asura. You are one of us. You should have come to me and told me what you suspected."

"I'm also IEPEU, and I was following protocol."

"Your protocol got him killed!"

His words were a slap in the face, and for the first time since she'd awoken inside me, my dragon bared her teeth at him. "Maybe you should read his damned confession, take a look at the evidence in his lab, and check out the ashes of the dead djinn whose souls he extracted before you point fingers. Your friend killed those innocent creatures. He almost killed me and all because he was sick of being your ancient sidekick. He wanted power. He wanted to be a god. He killed himself because he was ashamed—

because he got caught. Maybe you just didn't know him as well as you thought you did."

Vritra's expression shuttered, his anger retracting like a set of lethal claws. "You should have come to me," he said calmly. "I would have helped you contain him. If he was guilty, I would have helped you discover that, and maybe … maybe he would still be alive to receive his punishment. Your actions backed him into a corner. This is your fault. You were one of us …"

He stormed past me and down the stairs, leaving me with the sightless body of the sage and a twisting vortex of guilt in my chest.

17

Ice-cream was good. Ice-cream and chicken was a winning combination. My phone rang for the kazzilionth time and I hit silent.

This was *my* time. No death, no lies, no mysteries. Yeah, there were yamduth out to get me for whatever reason. Yeah, Paimon was shacking up with someone else. Yep, Vritra hated me and blamed me for the death of his friend. But right now, none of that mattered. All that mattered was the ice-cream, the bucket of chicken, and re-runs of *Buffy the Vampire Slayer*.

The cuff glared at me from the coffee table, daring me to put it back on. I'd found it there when I'd gotten back from the office. Paimon had even left a note which said, *Thank you,* and, *if you need me*. So I guessed he had his orb with the djinn souls and the answers he needed. It was truly over. I played with the chain around my neck. Should I put the cuff back on? Was I being unreasonable cutting all ties with him? Gah, it was just me making excuses to see him again. No. They cuff stayed off. For now.

A rap sounded at the door.

"Go away!"

"Open the damned door, before I break it down," Henna said.

Urgh. The daughter of my new enemy. "Have you come to kill me? Because if you have, you need to come back later, I'm in the middle of wallowing."

"I brought tequila."

"So, no stabby, stabby?"

"Not tonight."

I hopped off the sofa and let her in.

She held up a carrier bag. "Got lime and salt too."

"I have salt."

She shrugged. "Grab a couple of glasses, girl. We need to chat."

Five minutes and two shots later, Henna sat back with a drumstick. "You asked me why I killed the asura dad wanted to mate with."

"Yeah?"

"Well, I think it's time I told you why." She topped up her glass and drained it, forgoing the lime and salt. "My mother was an awesome woman. An asura, but not a dragon like Vritra, because there hadn't been anyone like him for a long time. Not till you. Anyway, he mated with her, and they were happy. Or at least I thought they were, but there were times I caught my mother looking sad, and when I asked why, she'd always make some bollocks excuse. Obviously, I didn't realize her excuses were bollocks at the time, being a child and all, I didn't even realize they were excuses, not until she got real sick. She was a seer, and she always said she'd seen something sad, and not to worry as it didn't concern us."

"I didn't know demi-gods could get sick."

Henna snorted. "Not the usual ailments, no. We didn't have those on the celestial plains, but demi-gods sometimes sicken and waste from afflictions of the heart or mind."

"And what was it with your mother? Heart or mind?"

She smiled wryly. "My mother died of a broken heart. I was old enough to understand by the time she was close to passing. She called me to her bedchamber, and she told me that she'd foreseen this day. She'd known she would die like this, but she'd chosen to love my father anyway, knowing full well that she would never hold all his heart. She made me swear an oath to guard my father's heart until a woman who could capture it whole entered his life. She told me that woman would have a dragon in her heart." She sat forward, poured another drink, and downed it. "I killed the asura woman to keep my oath." Her eyes misted. "I asked her to decline the mating offer, and she refused. I tried to change dad's mind, but he's a stubborn fool and wouldn't listen. He thought I needed a mother. He was about to tie himself to a woman who he would never love completely, and that woman, the fool that she was, was making the same mistake my mother had."

"So you killed her."

"Yeah. I did." She poured another drink and tipped that back too. "I'm not a monster, Carmella, but it helped that people saw me as such. It kept them at bay, until you came along. You were on dad's radar, and I almost killed you twice." She smiled. "Thank God I didn't succeed."

"Because I have a dragon inside me? You think I'm the woman your mother foretold?"

"I know it."

"No. I'm not your woman."

"No. You're his. I know my father, and he's never been this fixated on anyone before. If he had his way, he'd kidnap you and lock you in his penthouse suite where it's safe. You think it's easy for him, letting you roam free when there are yamduth after you? The first time you were attacked, at the Yaksha gathering, it took five of us to hold down his dragon, to prevent it coming for you."

"He shifted?"

"Nah, shifting is gradual, a fluid action. What he did was not shifting. He kinda burst into a dragon. We had to lock him up until he changed back."

"He came to see me the next day."

"Yeah, I was ready to slit your throat about that."

"Why didn't you come for me?"

"I was curious. And I was right to be. You found your dragon, or the dragon found you. What I'm trying to say in a roundabout way is that you have my blessing."

She thought I belonged with Vritra, and there was no denying the attraction, but it wasn't enough. Paimon's face flashed before my eyes, and my heart did its pitter-patter ache thing. Paimon may be gone, but my heart wasn't my own just yet.

"Thanks, but no thanks."

She frowned. "I know he's angry right now, but he will see sense. What happened wasn't your fault. He knows that, he's just hurting. Shukra was a close friend and one of the only people that really knew Vritra. The dragon that sired Vritra died a long time ago. All that's left of him are his bones, and Vritra refuses to part with those. I think, sometimes, when he's feeling particularly low or conflicted, he goes into the vault to speak to those bones."

Bones? The Yamduth had carried bone weapons. My brain was making strange connections. "I asked

Vritra what could cut through dragon armor, and he said there was always something. He didn't tell me what, but the Yamduth on the tram were carrying bone swords. And you guys defended me hardcore, so I assume bone can cut through dragon armor."

"Dragon bone. I'm certain they had dragon bone. Father probably didn't think it was likely they'd get hold of any. It's very rare. Aside from Father, there have only been a handful of asura who could shift into dragon form, and they all died millennia ago. Dragon bone coated with the blood of the target is even more lethal. Being reapers probably gives them access to resources we know nothing about and …" Her eyes widened. "But you don't think they got it from any old resource do you? You think they got the bones from the vault? You think Shukra gave them the bones." She sat up. "He has access to the vault, and so do I. There are only three keys. I'll have to go back and check the vault."

"But why would he order a hit on the yaksha? He didn't mention them in his note."

She shrugged. "If he was about to commit suicide he probably wasn't thinking straight."

There was more to this. Things just didn't add up properly. "Why go after me again? No. It still doesn't make sense."

"I get what you're saying. It just doesn't add up, does it? Look, Father can't know about this, not until we have all the facts. He's hurting right now, and if we're going to inflict more pain, we need to be sure it's unavoidable."

A hollow pit opened up inside me. "How bad is Vritra?"

"Locked away in his suite. He hasn't eaten or drunk anything all day."

Oh, God. He was in pain, and he blamed me. I buried my head in my hands. "You think … you think you can take me to him?"

Henna smiled and her face lit up. "Fucking hell, I thought you'd never ask."

THE PENTHOUSE SUITE was shrouded in darkness, the only illumination filtered in from between the slats in the vertical blinds covering the floor to ceiling windows.

I padded further into the room, my shoes sinking into the plush carpet.

"Vritra?"

No answer, but he was here. My body was thrumming with awareness of his presence. The sofas were dark, shadowy lumps. Was he sitting in one of the chairs? I moved farther into the room.

"Vritra, it's Carmella."

Heat caressed my back, and my dragon stretched as warm breath stirred the hairs at the top of my head.

"Don't you know it's dangerous to enter a dragon's den without invitation?" His voice was gravelly, like calloused fingers running across sensitized flesh.

I moistened my lips. "Henna said you hadn't eaten anything. You must be hungry."

His low rumbling chuckle raised gooseflesh across my skin.

"Yes. I'm hungry all right."

And then he was touching me, yanking me toward him, my back to his chest—hands caressing and kneading my hips and my breasts, thumbs rolling my hard nipples through the thin fabric of my shirt and bra. I couldn't breathe. No, I *was* breathing but it was too shallow and too fast. My head swam with sensations. My body was lit up, sensitized and hungry for more. His arousal pressed into the small of my back. It was time to pull away and put some distance between those clever hands and my eager body, but my dragon had other ideas and pressed against him, reveling in his heat. His lips and tongue claimed my neck. The world didn't matter when he sucked on my flesh like that. A whimper, a moan. Me. That was me. What was I doing?

He was supposed to be upset. This didn't feel like upset. He cupped my groin, his fingers rubbing against the growing heat and matching the throb of my desire. No. This wasn't why I'd come to see him. A bestial growl vibrated in his chest as if to shut down my thoughts. No thinking, woman, just feeling.

This wasn't the Vritra I knew. This was someone else … something else. This was the dragon, and it wanted my dragon. And from the way my power was pulsing, it wanted him too.

I tried to pull away "We should talk."

He lifted me off the ground and carried me across the room, pushing me up against the cool wall. His fingers gripped my hips and tugged. Fuck, I wanted him inside, me. No … Not me, my dragon. My dragon wanted this. *She* wanted him. And he was grinding up against me, his huge, hard cock rubbing against me. I was swollen with need—pulsing, wet, and ready.

I pushed into him, almost losing control. Dammit. No. This wasn't what I wanted. This was *her*—the dragon inside. She wanted Vritra, and he wanted her. Not me.

Never me.

I twisted in his grasp—my asura power lending me the strength. "No. Not this." I shoved him back, but it was like shoving a solid brick wall. He was immovable.

"You want me, Miss Hunter. I can smell it."

Fucking supernaturals and their super senses. "My dragon wants you, but *I* don't."

He blinked down at me in the gloom, the whites of his eyes gleaming in the moonlight, his savage face in shadow. He reached up to run the pad of his thumb over my lips. Oh, please … don't … God. My mouth parted, and my tongue flicked out to lick him. His body tensed, and a low moan tore from his throat. My core tightened.

"You are the dragon," he said roughly. "The dragon is you."

Our gazes locked, and he pressed his thumb to my lips. My control broke, and I took it into my mouth, sucking hard and tasting the salt on his skin.

"Fucking hell." His voice was an aroused rasp, and then his thumb was gone and his mouth was on mine—tongue tangling, mouth crushingly raw and violent. The scent of cinnamon filled my head as his hand tore at my leggings and slipped down into my panties. His finger slipped into my wetness. Ah, yes. Oh, fuck yes. He played me, and I moved with him. My dragon took over. There was no thought, only sensation, taste and smell and touch. The thick pile of the carpet beneath me, his huge body covering mine, his fingers inside me, mouth on my nipples drawing a line from my core to my breasts. I wanted this. I wanted him inside me. My body craved him like the

Sahara craved the rain. It would be epic, primal, raw, and liberating, satisfying, but … it wouldn't mend my heart.

The tiny voice inside me, the one that loved to reason, screamed out to stop. Stop this now.

"Stop." I pushed at his shoulders.

Vritra went completely still. He raised his head, ember eyes glowing in the dark. "Stop?"

My chest heaved, every nerve vibrating with pleasure. "Stop. Please."

He was off me in an instant. "Fucking hell, Hunter." He had his back to me, his shoulders rising and falling rapidly. And then he strode off into the bedroom.

Breathing shallow and fast, I pulled myself off the floor, adjusted my clothing, and then cautiously followed. The door to his bedroom was open, and a quick peek showed it to be empty, but the sound of running water drifted from the partially open en suite bathroom door. He was taking a shower.

My feet, treacherous things that they were, carried me to the ajar doorway. He was visible, his body obscured behind frosted glass, but still. There was no steam. He was taking a cold shower.

Oh, man. I could so do with one of those. I could climb in with him. Finish what we'd started.

Fucking hell! What was wrong with me?

The shower shut off.

Shit.

I legged it back to the main room and waited. I'd come here to talk to him, to resolve the issue of Shukra and get him to eat something, and I was damned if I was leaving without having done that.

Two minutes later, Vritra sauntered into the main room, naked except for a darned towel around his hips. What was he trying to do to me?

I turned away. "Can you please put on some clothes?"

"Well, seeing as you're not interested, it shouldn't matter."

I blew out a breath. "Look, it's not that simple."

"It's simple enough, you either want me or you don't. And for a good few minutes there, you wanted me very much."

I still did, but damned if I was going to fall into the trap of thinking with my vajayjay. "Just because we *could* have sex, it doesn't mean we *should*."

He snorted. "What did you come here for, Miss Hunter? Truly? Did you come to pet the poor sad dragon who just lost his best friend? Did you want to make him feel better? Is that why you came?"

He padded over, his eyes gleaming dangerously, and my body went into melt-down mode, because damn that guy rippled when he moved.

He stopped a foot away and leaned in. "I'll let you in on a little secret. Fucking you *would* have made me feel a whole lot better."

Shit, I was wet again. "I should go." I made to move past him

He side-stepped and blocked me. His breath was warm on my face. "Next time you walk into my suite, be prepared to be fucked. Hard."

Oh, God. I slipped around him and barreled to the door, before my dragon could take over and make me do something I'd regret.

18

The take-out menus were on the table, the flat was clean, and the sheets on the sofa-bed had been changed. Aaron would be arriving in an hour, maybe less. God, how long since we'd last seen each other? Four, maybe five months? My other bestie, Aaron, was my go-to-guy, the brother I'd have chosen if given the chance, and the only guy that had ever shared my bed without any hanky panky.

Tonight would be epic: chatting, take-out, and maybe a movie. But probably just a whole load of catching up. He'd get all big-brother protective over the Yamduth being after me. Although, maybe they weren't out to get me any longer. Henna's trip to the vault confirmed that some bones were missing. If

Shukra had been the one behind the hit, surely being dead cancelled out the bounty? Shukra must have hired the Yamduth to kill the Yaksha and then come after me. But no yaksha souls had been found at Shukra's residence, and there was no real motive to want me dead. So yeah, things still didn't add up. I'd agreed to hold off on reporting this to the IEPEU, to give Vritra time to grieve before they were crawling all over his vault looking for evidence in the Yamduth case. The cuff was still sitting on the coffee table. Without giving myself too much time to think, I popped it back on again.

Just in case.

My phone rang. Eeep, that was probably Aaron saying he was at the station. Ooh, maybe I should go meet him. The phone rang again.

Crap, I probably should answer it first. "Aaron?"

"Carm, babe, I have some bad news."

My heart crawled into my boots. "You can't make it."

"I was half way there, and I got a call. I've had to turn back. Sweets, I promise I'm gonna wrap this shit up and get down there to see you ASAP."

"Yeah. 'Kay."

"Love you."

"Love you too."

He hung up. Do not burst into tears. I sniffed. Gosh, I needed to man up. Urvashi was on a date. Banner wasn't answering his phone, and Honey was on pack business. That left Vritra, who wanted to fuck me, and Paimon, who couldn't. Wait. What was Henna up to tonight? I tugged out my phone to find out, and it buzzed in my hand. The number was withheld.

"Hello?"

"Miss Hunter." The High Witch's cool refined voice filtered down the line. "We need to speak in person."

"I assume this is about Karen, right?"

"You assume correctly. May I send a car?"

As much as I wanted to tell her where to shove her car, I couldn't turn my back on this responsibility. "Yeah, sure."

"It'll be with you in fifteen minutes."

Well, looked like the moping and take-away would have to wait.

FASHION MODEL HENRY led me into the library and then closed the door behind me. The room was dimly lit, and the tip of the High Witch's up-do was visible over the top of the wingback facing away from me.

"Please come take a seat, Miss Hunter."

Parking my butt in the wingback across from her, I crossed my arms and waited. She looked even younger today, and if not for the silver of her hair and the tired look in her pale eyes, I'd have pegged her for no more than thirty-five years old.

The High Witch sighed. "I believe my words wounded you gravely the other day."

"Well, there aren't many people who take kindly to being called an abomination."

"Please, accept my apology. It was simply the nature of the spell. The intent had to be strong, and in order to bar you from the skein, we were forced to use explicit language as to why."

"Well, some warning would have been nice."

"In hindsight, yes, that would have been wise."

I just wanted to get this over with and go home. Being targeted for death twice in the same month was beginning to take its toll. Being given power then having it taken away was beginning to get old. *I* was beginning to get fucking old. "So, you wanted to see me about the Daayan? Have you traced her?"

"No. But we've found a way to trace her, and we need your help."

"Tell me what you need."

"The Daayan is connected to the skein."

"What? You have to be kidding me."

She pursed her lips. "I wish I was. This relates directly to the witch's oath you took—the knowledge that the Daayan were once human women chosen from each of the original witch bloodlines—so you will not disclose this fact. Only the High Witches are aware of it. We discovered the connection this morning. It's tentative, but there, and not surprising since the vengeful spirit now belongs to the demon, and the demon is somehow able to grant us access to the skein."

"There are a lot of somehows and maybes floating about. If I didn't know better, I'd say you really didn't have a clue how this all works."

"And you'd be correct in your assumption. The Daayan, the demon, and the original witches are all tales that have been passed down from High Witch to High Witch, word of mouth for generations. How much is true, and how much has been altered by time is something we can only guess at."

"But you told me."

She smiled softly. "Yes. What a rebel I am."

Was that a twinkle of mischief in her eye? "So, what happens now? Can we track her using her connection to the skein?"

"Yes. I can. But I will need you with me. Once we find her, we must open the doorway and send her back, together."

"Just the two of us?"

"Yes. Just the two of us."

"And what about my magick? I'll need access to the skein for that."

The High Witch nodded. "It's something the High Witch council was aware of when we barred you, and they have given me authority to lift the bar for a short period of time."

"How short?"

"Five minutes."

Wow, they *really* didn't trust me. "You're not making this easy on yourselves, are you?"

She swallowed and glanced down at her lap. "I'm going to tell you something now, Miss Hunter. Something that I should only reveal under oath, but consider it an act of good faith that I am sharing this information without sealing your tongue."

The woman certainly had a way with words. "I'm listening."

"Our connection to the skein is unravelling. We're running out of time. Witches are reporting loss of access, spotty access, and some have even claimed that spells they did days ago have unraveled."

Oh, shit. "The agreement is breaking down."

She nodded, her expression solemn. "We must find her and return her, or magick will be lost to us, and, Miss Hunter, that means retroactive loss."

"You mean old spells will be undone?"

"Exactly."

How many people had used magick to fix a problem, to survive, to heal or cure a loved one. How many buildings had been forged using magickal tech created by Brahma Corp. With our connection gone, all that would crumble. I couldn't let that happen.

"How will you do it? Lift the bar?"

She held up a tiny tape recorder. "The reversal chant is on here. It's been sped up to last only a second, but the essence is the same, so it should work?"

"Should?"

"The theory is sound."

Great. We were going on theory. "Shouldn't we test it out just in case?"

"It's a one shot deal, Miss Hunter. I play it and it works, but then it's useless for a second use. Barring a witch from the skein is difficult. To you, it probably seemed like we spoke a few words and it was done, but the witches who spoke that spell spent days chanting, believing in their words and honing their intent. The word abomination was their anchor for belief that what they were asking for was indeed right. The same goes for a reversal. We just don't have the time or the energy to recreate it right now."

Theory it was then. "So, where is she?"

"We're working to get a lock on her. As soon as we do, I will call you. Will you be there, Miss Hunter?"

"I'll be there."

What choice did I have?

19

Table was set, flat was clean, take two on having friends over. Saturday nights were no longer about going out and getting pissed. I tucked a stray strand of hair behind my ear. The rest was piled up on my head in a messy knot. Urvashi exited the bathroom, adjusting her knickers.

I bit back an amused smile. "What is wrong with you tonight? Hungry bum syndrome?"

She winced. "New thong, but I think it's a little tight." Her eyes widened. "Oh, no. My butt is getting fat." She spun to give me a view of her pert backside. "Is it getting fat? It is, isn't it?"

I cocked my head. "You know what, now that you mention it..."

He bottom lip trembled.

"It looks the fucking same as it always does."

"Phew!" She pressed her hand to her chest. "So, what were you saying about the High Witch before my arse decided to eat my knickers?"

"You're wearing a thong, so you're practically force feeding your butt."

She growled in exasperation, tugging at her pants. "Shoddy, discount lingerie. You know what? I'm just gonna take them off. Fuck it." She headed back to the bathroom.

A knock at the door signaled the arrival of another guest. Henna stood on the doorstep, bottle of tequila in her hands, and Honey stood behind her with a box of donuts held out like a peace offering. The girls traipsed in, and before I could close the door, Victor made it to the top of the stairs followed closely by Banner. Melody and I'd made enough of a case to get the Rakshasa released. They'd been literal puppets under Shukra's control, and the IEPEU had agreed to drop the charges.

The gang was here. It was time to get the party started.

Okay, so it wasn't a party, more of a noisy get together with food and copious amounts of alcohol. Banner flirted with Honey, but soon cottoned on that she only had eyes for Victor, who only had eyes for the floor. Shit. We really hadn't had a chance to discuss the whole, hey-so-you-tried-to-kill-me thing. Well, no time like the present.

"Victor, can you give me a hand in the kitchen?" Right, so it was barely a couple of meters from the dining area, but still.

Victor joined me behind the counter but didn't look me in the eye.

I ducked my head to try and capture his gaze. "How have you been?"

He snorted. "Wracked with guilt. You?"

"Tired, to be honest. Life of a superhero sucks."

He chuckled. "How can you be so okay with this?"

"With what?"

He looked up, locking gazes with me. "I tried to kill you."

"Okay. True. But … you didn't. Plus, you were under evil Shukra's control, and even though you weren't entirely yourself, you tried to protect me by hiding me in the apartments under Soho."

He looked away. "Urvashi said the same thing. She came to see me at the kitchen. But I should have gone for help sooner. Told someone about the blackouts. Something. It could all have been avoided."

"Or Shukra would have replaced you with another rakshasa who wouldn't have given a fuck about me and killed me."

His head whipped round, his attention back on me.

"So, you see, you kinda saved my life."

He offered me a wry smile. "No, Carmella. You saved your own life. You knit yourself back together using your power."

"Power I would never have discovered if I hadn't been on the brink—" I waved a hand in the air, cutting myself off. "You know what, we could do this all day, but it doesn't change the fact that you are my friend and there is nothing to forgive." I shoved a drink into his hand. "Now go eat, drink, and be merry, and for goodness sake, flirt with the hot yaksha before she gets a complex."

He finally cracked a genuine smile and rejoined the others at the table.

Henna held up a carrier bag. "Hunter, chop up the lime while you're there." She passed the bag to Banner who brought it over.

Shot glasses were arranged on the table.

Banner grabbed a knife. In the glare of the overhead light, his skin looked pale and drawn. Were those dark circles under his eyes?

"What?" he asked. "Wait, I know. You've finally succumbed to my manly beauty."

I couldn't exactly tell him he looked ill now, could I? "You wish."

He pouted and handed me the knife. "Hey, what are you up to tomorrow evening?"

"No plans, why?"

"Pizza and a movie at mine?" He rolled his eyes. "Hannah is out of town, and so I'm fending for myself, plus, the house is kinda creepy without her. I could grab a date and do the whole Casanova thing, but, to be honest, I'm not in the mood."

Was this a ploy to get me alone? Was he still hoping we'd be more than friends? There was nothing in his expression or in his eyes to suggest such a thing, and no warning from my gut.

"Did you just admit that you need me to come over to hold your hand while your housekeeper's away?"

He grinned sheepishly. "If you tell anyone, I'll turn you into a toad."

I snorted. "Sure, I'll come babysit."

"I'll pick you up at six then?"

"Awesome." I began to slice. "Grab me a bowl, would you?"

"Where?" He started opening cupboards.

"Forgotten already?" I glanced over my shoulder. "The cupboard above the—" Pain sliced through my finger. "Fuck."

"What?"

"I cut my finger."

Banner grabbed a wad of kitchen towel and wrapped it around my bleeding appendage.

"You okay?" Honey asked.

"Will be in a moment. It'll heal."

“She’s a bleeder, that one,” Henna said to Victor.

Victor’s face paled, and Urvashi snorted.

“Too soon?” I asked Victor.

He shook his head in despair, and the tension was defused.

Banner released the pressure on my finger and removed the paper towel.

I wiggled my hand. “See, all healed.” Grabbing the non-bloody limes, I joined the others at the table.

“So, what did the High Witch want?” Urvashi asked.

Oh, yeah, I’d started to tell her but had been interrupted by her pants.

“The High Witch was in touch?” Banner asked.

“Yeah. She wants me to help her catch Karen. They figured out some way to trace her, and she wanted me on standby to help send the Daayan back.”

Banner’s lips tightened. “The Daayan desperately needs to go back. Poor Karen. I can’t even imagine what she’s going through with that thing inside her.”

He didn’t know what the Daayan really was, or why she’d been able to possess a witch.

“We should play a drinking game,” Urvashi said.

Henna downed another shot. "I don't need a game to get me drinking." She winked.

A breeze blew through the room, and a chill caressed the back of my neck.

Paimon?

Honey's gaze was fixed over my shoulder. "Um, you have a guest."

I inhaled and exhaled through my nose. "Excuse me, guys." I pushed my chair back and turned to face Paimon.

"Carmella, may we speak in private?"

I walked past him and swept an arm toward the bathroom. "Step into my office."

I shut the door behind us and leaned against it—heart pounding to be this close to him again. "What can I do for you?"

His gaze flicked to my wrist, and a small smile tugged on his lips. "You have it on again."

"For now. Look, Paimon, I have guests so …"

"Yes. Of course. The orb the IEPEU handed over has been examined, and there are only two djinn souls contained within. If this Shukra was collecting the souls to create this amrit he speaks of but no amrit was located, then where are the rest of the souls?"

"Oh, shit."

"The families of the missing djinn are waiting for their loved one's souls to be released into their care so final rites can be performed. Amon and I have managed to stall, but the council is pressing for answers. I won't be able to stall for much longer. I need answers or else I need the rest of those souls."

"I've had a bad feeling about this since we found Shukra's dead body. There are too many holes in this wrap-up, and this is another one to add to the list. I also have a bad feeling that we may not be getting the answers anytime soon."

"The deal was that you deliver to us the kidnapper and either our missing djinn or an answer as to what became of them. We have only two souls, and the fate of the other twenty are unaccounted for. If you'd found this amrit then that may have been answer enough."

Oh, fuck.

"I will stall for as long as I can, but Carmella, even I have my limitations. There are members of the council, factions of djinn, itching to move into this realm. They want to expand and claim territory and turn your world into an extension of our own. Any excuse to reopen talks of invasion would be welcome."

His cerulean eyes were tight with concern, his expression strained, and I ached to smooth away the worry lines on his forehead. As if sensing my thoughts and desires, he took a step closer, slipping into my personal space.

My blood fizzed. "How's Alara?"

He closed his eyes and took a step back. "She is well. Thank you."

I pressed my lips together. "Great. You should go. I'll let Parker know what you found, and we'll get on it." I nodded curtly.

He tried to lock gazes with me, but I fixed my attention on the rim of the bathroom sink.

I caught movement in the periphery of my vision. His hand coming up to caress my face.

"Carmella, I—"

"Should go. You should go now." I met his gaze steadily. "I'll let you know what we find."

He reined it in, taking his cue from me. “Thank you.”

Was he thanking me for looking into things, or for preventing him from losing himself again? He smiled tenderly, and then he was gone.

A rap on the door. “Carmella, your phone is buzzing,” Urvashi said.

I opened the door and grabbed it from her. “Hi.”

“Miss Hunter,” the High Witch said. “It’s time.”

20

"So, we need to look into this," I said to Melody on the phone after filling her in on Paimon's visit. "Maybe search Shukra's place again. Those souls have to be somewhere. If not, then the djinn may still be alive."

"I'll get down there first thing in the morning," Melody said. "And Carmella, we need to wrap up this Yamduth case too. We need to find out who's responsible for the hit. Murdoch is getting antsy that his perfect record will be tarnished."

It was on the tip of my tongue to tell her what we'd found out about the dragon bones, Shukra, and the vault, but I'd made Henna a promise to hold off until we'd tied up the loose ends—until we'd figured out where the yaksha souls, he'd apparently harvested, were and what his motive for still wanting me dead was.

"I'm working on it. I'll meet you at Shukra's in the morning." I clattered down the steps from my flat. The High Witch had asked me to meet her at the Piccadilly Circus Underground station in half an hour. Naturally the gang had wanted to come, but there was nothing they could do to help. This was a two man job. Locate and banish. Hopefully, I'd be back in time to join the party.

Hopefully.

I hit the pavement just as the headlights of a car swept across the back of the bakery. It came to a halt. The lights died and a door slammed. A figure came racing toward me. A familiar face, a much loved grin, and then I was swept off my feet and into a bear hug worthy of a bear.

"Babe." Aaron rocked me from side to side then popped me back on my feet.

"You made it." I couldn't believe he was actually here.

"I said I would. Had to steal a car, but." He shrugged.

"Whose is it?"

"Loki's"

"No!" Loki was, well, he'd been my first mega crush. An independent witch from another reality, he'd helped us to stop the void and been recruited by the IEPEU alongside Aaron. It had been a long time since I'd seen that charismatic man.

"Where are you off to?" Aaron asked.

Oh, shit. How to explain this? "To meet the Mayfair High Witch at the Piccadilly Circus Underground station so we can corner a witch possessed by a vengeful spirit from another dimension and send it back."

Aaron blinked down at me. "Okay. Let's go." He strode toward his car.

I loved that it was so easy with Aaron. "You don't need to come. The High Witch and I can manage."

"I'm sure you can, but it doesn't hurt to have a little back up. He gave me his signature dimpled grin, and, man, was I a sucker for that grin. I could never say no to Aaron.

"Fine."

Aaron opened the passenger door to the car. A very expensive car by the looks of it. I slid onto the plush leather, and the door closed smoothly. Wow, leg room galore. Aaron jumped in and the engine purred—like literally purred—to life.

"Loki is gonna kill you."

Aaron smiled. "He'll never know."

Then we were off, sailing down the street into the city night.

GRIMY POSTERS DECORATED the cracked tiled walls, and the stench of urine drifted up to meet us as we descended into the underground. I'd dressed in boots, jeans and a black T-shirt for this adventure. Aaron was sleek and panther-like in his dark clothing. Together, we blended into the night. He probably had a dagger or two strapped to his person. Maybe a gun? The guy rarely went anywhere without a mini arsenal.

His hair was slicked back from his forehead, making him look older, and right now, he had that focused, on-the-look-out-for-trouble glint in his eye. It was his assassin-mode face, although he wasn't an assassin any longer—he was IEPEU.

The turnstiles were practically hanging off their moorings. Aaron leapt over and reached across to give me a hand. With an impish grin, I vaulted across to land at his side. Asura power came with strength and agility.

"Show off," Aaron said. "Come on. Where did she say she'd meet you?"

"Just here, by the barriers." Farther steps awaited beyond to take us down into the bowels of a travel system very few sane people employed. "They should never have reopened these."

"I know. They're a death trap."

"So, where have you been? Where is this new branch of IEPEU?"

His eyes did the shifty thing they do when he was mentally sifting through information. He was deciding what he could tell me.

"It's coastal," he said.

"That's it? That's all you can tell me?"

He winced. "Have I told you I love you?"

"Aaron, seriously? How can you have a relationship or a life when everything you do is classified?"

His expression sobered, his eyes darkening. "You can't."

"So, why do it?"

His lips thinned. "Because somebody has to." He clasped his hands together. "Look, Carmella, like my daddy once said, with great power, comes great responsibility."

"Your daddy said that?"

"Uh-huh."

"Are you sure it wasn't Spiderman's uncle?"

He gave me a faux puzzled look. "Hang on … I may be getting confused here."

A scream echoed up the steps.

Aaron's body tensed. "This place is crawling with vamps. It could be a trap, a way to lure us down there. They probably smell the blood coursing through our veins."

"Or it could be someone in need of help."

His lips curved in his signature, roguish smile. “Fancy taking your asura powers for a spin?”

Did I just.

Another scream bounced its way up the steps. Fuck it. I broke into a run, Aaron hot on my heels. Farther into the depths of the underground we went: flickering anemic lights, patches of absolute darkness, and that God-awful stench of waste. How the fuck could the vamps stand it down here with their super senses. The *whoosh* and *clatter* of a train carried through the brickwork as it made its departure, and then we were hitting the dead escalators and delving even farther into the complex. Another scream drifted up to greet us.

Someone was having a party, and not the kind with candy and streamers.

“Please, please, don’t. We’ve changed our minds. Here, take your money.”

We hit the bottom of the escalators, and the tunnel ahead came into view. A group of vamps had a woman and her teenaged son surrounded. Five on two, so not cool. Five vamps against two humans? Triple uncool.

"Oi, back off," Aaron said striding forward.

The vamps turned to face us, and a third figure came into a view. It was a barely conscious male, laying on the floor with a needle and blood bag still attached to his jugular.

What the fuck?

"Please, you have to help him." The woman implored us.

The boy had to be no older than fourteen or fifteen, and he was skin and bones. The vamps wouldn't be getting much out of him. It looked like the dude on the floor was the dad, selling his blood for cash to feed his family.

"Look, take the bag and go," Aaron said calmly. "Fair deal and all that."

The man on the ground moaned.

"Fuck you," one of the vamps said. "This is our territory. You stay, you pay. You pass through, you pay. You set foot in it, you motherfucking pay."

I joined Aaron, leaning in to stage a whisper. "Someone's been watching too many gangster movies."

"Bitch," the vamp said.

I pressed my hand to my heart. “Wow, how original. I’m impressed.”

Vamps were fast and their fangs were sharp, but their bodies were dead and in a constant state of decomposition. So, a hard enough swing with a bat, and their heads popped off. Shame I hadn’t thought to bring one with me. Ooh, or a Sun shot. The IEPEU had a bunch of those beauties—they gave off electromagnetic radiation that mimicked the sun’s rays. Instant *poof.* It was all right though, because with my new found asura strength, I should be able to just yank his head off.

I cocked my head. “Can I have the mouthy one?”

“Be my guest,” Aaron said.

We advanced, and the Vamp reached into the voluminous folds of his tacky trench and pulled out a fucking gun

The others followed suit.

Well, that changed the game. Aaron’s fingers twitched to draw his weapon, but with five guns trained on us, it was a bad move.

"You, silver head, come over here." Mouthy vamp jerked his head in my direction. "Get that tight ass over here."

"You gonna suck on her Brendan, are ya?" one of his weasel-faced compadres asked.

Seriously, they got to pick and choose their skins, so I could only assume it had been slender pickings at the morgue that day. Brendan, the obvious ring leader, grinned, showcasing receding gums. He obviously hadn't been taking great care of his meat suit.

"Fuck yeah, I'm gonna suck on her, straight from the motherfucking vein."

"Aw, man. If Garnet finds out, we're dead," one of the guys in the shadows said.

Weasel dude burst into crazy hyena giggles. "You twat, we can't get deader than this."

"Fuck Garnet," Brendan said. "I'm sick of being his errand boy. It's about time someone—" His eyes grew wide, and then he toppled forward onto his face, the reason why was evident when he hit the ground. A slender arrow protruded from his back, and then the vamp exploded into ash.

Aaron grabbed my hand and tugged me back. “That’s a Sun Spear.”

“Spear? Looks like an arrow to me.”

“It is. They just call it a spear. The arrowhead detonates inside the vamp sending out UV radiation that mimics the sun. Fuck.”

The remaining vamps hit the dirt in bows of supplication, and the human woman fell to the ground to nurse her husband. But the main attraction was the guy striding toward us from the depths of the tunnel—the reason for all the bowing and scraping, and fuck, he was huge. His hair was long, coming to just above his shoulders and was tucked behind his ears, and his face was chiseled but covered in a neat goatee. Hip-hugging jeans and pec-loving T-shirt completed the ensemble.

His gaze was fixed on us as he bridged the distance. “Apologies.” He stopped by the bowing vamps, pulled a Sun Shot from a holster at his hip, and blasted them into oblivion one by one in quick succession. “I’m sorry you had to see that.” He crouched by the trembling woman. “You have my gratitude for the blood, and my sincere apology for the manner in which it was obtained." He carefully extracted the needle from the man's neck, nicked his own thumb with a fang, and wiped his blood over the wound.

The woman began to sob. "Please. Don't hurt us."

"I have no intention of harming you. Leave this place now."

The woman scrambled up, dragged her barely stable husband to his feet, and slipped under his arm. The son took the other side, and they staggered past us.

"Where did you get the weapons?" Aaron asked.

The vampire turned the Sun Shot over in his hand. "This? A friend."

Aaron's eyes narrowed. "What friend?"

The vamp, Garnet, I presumed, stepped out of the tunnel. "That is none of your business. Now, I've apologized for the actions of my soldiers. It's so hard to get good help nowadays. Everyone either wants to cheat or double cross. All I ask for is some clean, decent business. Bag of blood for cash. Not too hard to fathom, but I had a suspicion Brendan and his lot were taking liberties. Sipping from the vein." His gaze fell to me, and he licked his lips. "Although I can see the allure on this occasion."

Aaron tensed. "Keep your eyes off her."

Garnet held up his hands. "I'm a businessman. I only take what's given freely in trade. Do you want to trade?" he asked me.

"No, thanks."

"So, travelers then?" He looked us up and down. "No, too well dressed to be using the death trains. So, that begs the question. What *are* you doing down here?"

"Waiting for a friend," Aaron said.

"Has your friend got a name?"

I smiled slyly. "That is none of your business."

He chuckled.

The sound of footsteps echoed down around us, and my scalp prickled. I glanced over my shoulder to see the High Witch walking toward us. She was dressed more casually than I'd ever seen her. Her youthful body was encased in neat slacks and a scoop neck shirt. Her silver-gray hair was pulled in a French braid. But her youthful face was turned toward

Garnet, her lips parted in surprise, or awe, I couldn't quite determine.

"Elora," Garnet said softly.

The High Witch cleared her throat. "It's good to see you, Garnet. I'd heard rumors that you were operating your business in the underground these days."

Something dark and intimate flitted across his face. "You've been keeping tabs on me?"

"Hardly," she scoffed.

"So *you're* the friend they've been waiting for. And what brings you out of your tower of solitude and down into the depths of depravity?"

"We're looking for a witch possessed by a vengeful spirit."

Garnets eyes narrowed. "Witches can't be possessed."

The High Witch strode toward us and then past us into the tunnel. "This spirit isn't from our reality and, therefore—"

"Bullshit," Garnet snapped. "You're lying. But heck. What's new there?"

Okay, so there was some history here, but wow, the Mayfair High Witch and a vampire? Seriously? This was one story I needed to hear.

Aaron and I exchanged glances, then ran to catch up to the odd pair.

Was it my imagination or was there a bounce in the High Witch's step? A flirtatious lilt to her voice?

I caught up to the High Witch. "How far in is she?"

"Platform one, I think." She tapped her ear. "Giselle, dear, are we still on track?" She nodded. "Uh-huh. Yes, please, dear. Tea would be lovely."

Garnet snorted.

"So," I drew out the syllable. "How do you know each other?"

"Ha!" Garnet barked.

"Shut up," the High Witch ordered.

He slid a sly glance my way.

Yeah, there was definitely a story here.

We took a left and spilled out onto the platform for the Baker Loo line.

"So, where is this witch?" Aaron asked.

A moan reverberated around the platform, and the lights went out.

"I think she heard us," Aaron said.

An orb of light appeared above us, casting enough illumination to allow us to avoid falling onto the tracks.

Leave. Go. Leave now.

"Karen, sweetheart, can you hear me?" the High Witch crooned. "Come out. You don't need to hide. We want to help you."

Karen doesn't want to come. Karen is with me.

"If that's the case, then let Karen speak for herself."

Silence, thick and ominous, pressed against us, and even the orb of light wasn't enough to alleviate the oppressive feeling.

"Karen?"

"I … I'm here. I'm all right. Please, just leave us alone."

I nudged the High Witch. "Is that her?"

"It certainly sounds like her, but the Daayan could be mimicking Karen's voice."

"Please, just leave us be, and we'll leave you be."

"We can't do that," the High Witch said. "The Daayan must go back from where she came. There is no other choice, and we will not stop until she is returned."

Home.

The word reverberated around us in the dark, sending shivers up my spine.

The High Witch jerked her head to the left. There was a pillar up ahead. Was she hiding behind there? The High Witch's slender hand slipped into mine. It was time. She locked gazes with me and held up the tiny recorder.

Now, she mouthed. And then she switched on the machine. A garbled message played for less than a second, and then the skein lit up in my mind's eyes. My threads flared to life as the connection was re-established.

The High Witch began to stride toward the pillar, taking me with her.

"*Fractum expellit tenebras lucem et de animabus*," she chanted.

I joined in the chant, focusing on opening the door—a maw like last time. Nothing happened. The

High Witch squeezed my hand. Come on, maw, come the fuck on. We rounded the pillar to face … nothing.

Home.

The voice filled the air again and then a chuckle followed. The ball of light was overhead now. Where was the voice coming from? The High Witch released my hand and broke the chant.

I glanced at her. “What? What happened?”

She looked up at the wall behind the pillar, and I followed her gaze to see a large air vent. A final chuckle drifted down to us through the grill, and then there was silence.

WE’D BEEN DUPED, and the High Witch was furious. The incantation would have to be redone, and time was running out.

Aaron pulled up outside my flat. The lights were still on upstairs. So, hopefully, the party was still going.

“You’re going to love everyone.” I unbuckled my seatbelt and reached for the door.

Aaron made no move to exit the vehicle.

"Aaron?"

He gave me an apologetic look.

I sighed. "You're not coming up are you?"

"No."

"It's about those damned weapons Garnet had, isn't it?"

"Yep."

"And you can't tell me any more than that."

"That's right."

My vision blurred, and he pulled me into a tight hug, pressing a kiss to the side of my head.

"You were amazing tonight," he said. "I'm so fucking proud of you, babe. Malina would be so proud of you."

Darn it, he was going to make me cry. "Don't leave it so long between visits next time, 'kay?"

"I promise. And you promise to keep doing what you're doing. It suits you, Carm."

"I promise." I climbed out into the warm night.

Seeing him had been amazing, but in a way it had made things worse by reminding me what I was missing. The amber lights spilling from my window soothed me, assuring me that there were others waiting for me—new friends, but no less important.

Something moved in the periphery of my vision. No. Just shadows. But still. Best get inside and cozy up to the tequila. I could put the world to rights tomorrow.

21

Was it tomorrow already? I rolled onto my back and opened my eyes. No. The room was still dark. Still night time. So, why the fuck was I awake? What time had everyone left? One in the morning. Yeah, and my mouth tasted all furry. Being an asura meant no hangover, but you didn't escape the furry alcohol tongue. Yuck.

Okay, time to go back to sleep.

My power resisted—alert and way too awake.

Danger.

I kept my breath even but opened up my senses to scan the room. Shadows, shadows everywhere. The one by the kitchen counter … Had that just moved? And then it detached itself from the larger clump of darkness and advanced toward me. My body flooded with adrenaline, and I was up and in a defensive crouch before I could think.

The key must be eliminated.

Oh, fuck me sideways. “Karen. You don’t have to do this. You can control it. Just try.”

Karen is sleeping. Karen doesn’t like to see the blood.

Oh, shit.

Why hadn’t I considered that she might come after me? She probably followed me home. Darn London traffic and the snail’s pace.

The Daayan levitated across the room toward me. Had she been the shadow outside the flat? Why wait so long to attack? Everyone had left at least an hour ago.

“You don’t want to kill me.” At least I hoped she didn’t. “You aren’t a killer.”

She laughed. *You don’t know what I am.*

“Actually, I do, but I can’t say it out loud because I took a witch’s oath.”

She cocked her head, her scraggy hair falling to obscure half her face. She stared at me with one demon black eye. *She told?*

"Yeah, she did."

And you still wish to send me back? Back to torment and darkness?

When she put it like that, it sounded pretty unreasonable, but then … "You ate people."

Her head lolled back. *Flesh of my flesh, filled with flesh. Filled with life.*

O-kay. "Look. What happened to you was awful, but if we don't send you back then bad shit is gonna happen to a whole lot of people."

And I should care for these people? Care for those who cared not for me?

She had a point. Fuck. I couldn't send her back without the High Witch and the damned incantation. My connection to the skein had snapped as soon as the five minutes were up.

The pearl? I could trap her in it, but where the fuck was it?

She floated closer.

Banner had given it to me, I'd taken it off him and …

The witch lunged, her hands outstretched like desperate claws. I dove out the way, hitting the floor, rolling to my feet and legging it to the key bowl by the front door. I grabbed the pearl and spun just as she rushed me. She hit me hard, and my grip on the pearl loosened, sending it clattering across the floor.

Fuck, fuck. I smashed a fist into the side of her head. She swayed, and I followed up with an uppercut to send her flying. Sorry, Karen.

The damned pearl. There, glinting in the moonlight, by the window. I lunged for it, just as she leapt at me from the side. She caught my legs, throwing off my trajectory. I hit the carpet hard, fingers making contact with the pearl only to flick it under the radiator beneath the window.

Shitting hell.

She landed on my back and pain tore across my scalp as she yanked my head back with a fist full of hair.

The key must die.

My throat began to close up, tongue and neck straining as she tugged. She was gonna rip off my fucking head.

Glass exploded into the room and a shadow figure, dark hair flying, attacked the Daayan. Karen's weight was knocked off me. I was free. The pearl. I needed to get the pearl. My hands skimmed across the floor beneath the radiator, catching mini dust bunnies, something squidgy, and urgh, had something just skittered over my hand? But I had the pearl. Jumping up, I joined the window smashing female in her grapple with the Daayan. We pinned her down, and I slammed the pearl against her forehead.

The Daayan's eyes widened and then she bucked. The pearl began to glow and then dulled. The darkness bled out of Karen's eyes, and her lids fluttered closed.

My savior jumped up and bolted for the door.

"Wait!"

She paused to glance over her shoulder. I knew that face: dark eyes, slender features, dark hair. It was the woman who'd been watching me in the bar. But it was more than that. I knew her from somewhere else,

I just couldn't quite put my finger on it. Her gaze dropped to my throat, and she took a step toward me.

I tensed. "Who are you? I know you …"

Headlights painted a path across the dark room, momentarily blinding me, and when I opened my eyes, the woman was gone.

MORNING ARRIVED TOO soon, and the idea of facing the day made my stomach turn. The fact that I'd been attacked in my own home made my head ache with the injustice of it all. Was it barely a few weeks ago when life had been mundane and kinda boring? Which idiot had wept for more? Yeah, the twit staring back at me from the bathroom mirror, that's who. I spat out the toothpaste and bared my teeth. Death had brushed its chilly hand across my forehead last night. I was lucky to be alive.

The woman who'd saved my arse was a mystery, the headlights that scared her away not so much. The witches tracking the Daayan had located Karen and sent back up. Too late though. If the mystery woman hadn't shown up, I'd be dead.

I dressed quickly and drained my coffee cup, the taste of toothpaste turning it into something entirely icky.

The pearl was with the High Witch, and they were working on the incantation to get me access to the skein long enough to send the Daayan back. A couple more days, and my obligation to the witches would be over. The only mystery left to solve now was the location of the rest of the missing djinn and yaksha souls. There was something eluding me, some clue I'd overlooked.

The door slammed behind me, and I clattered down the stairs. I had an appointment with Melody at Shukra's residence.

There had to be something we'd missed.

MELODY GREETED ME at the door, she was in plain clothes today—jeans, a cami top, and ballet flats, with a large bag slung over her shoulder.

"How you feeling?" she asked as she led me down the hallway.

"Okay, thanks to super healing. Not even a bruise. Any luck with identifying the woman I described?"

"Not yet, but if we've had dealings with her, she'll be in our database. It doesn't look like she wants to hurt you though, and it's likely she'll approach you again. You said she was watching you a week ago?"

"Yeah." We climbed the steps to Shukra's bedroom.

"Anything from Paimon? Timescale before they invade us? The council has been informed, and we have a contingency plan in motion, and an army of our own."

"We won't win, will we?"

She sighed. "It's unlikely, but we'll sure as hell try. Let's just hope it doesn't come to that."

"I haven't heard from him since he told me the orb only held two djinn souls. He's doing his best to stall."

“Then we need to do our best to get some damned answers.”

“Okay, we start in here.” She pulled a pair of latex gloves from her bag and handed them to me.

We split up and began combing the room. The wardrobes, the chest of drawers, we even moved the idol sitting on the rug in the corner and rolled the rug up to check the laminate underneath.

“The team scanned the walls for hidden safes,” Melody said. “Nothing.”

“We have to be missing something.”

Melody straightened and reached into her bag to pull out a folder. She flipped it open to reveal color shots of the crime scene, complete with Shukra’s dead body.

“Sometimes studying the scene through a lens helps,” she said passing the folder to me.

Shukra was sprawled on the ground as if he’d simply cut his wrists and dropped. His face was turned to the right, his right arm flung out in the same direction. It was almost as if he was reaching for something. Wait … He wasn’t reaching, he was pointing. I turned to glance behind me, at the corner that Shukra had been pointing. It was empty, but the object that had occupied the space was placed to one side.

The idol.

"What is it?" Melody asked.

"Is it okay to break stuff?"

She frowned. "What?"

I showed her the picture. "Look. It looks like he's pointing at the idol."

Melody grabbed the idol and dropped it on the laminate floor. "Oops." It crashed to the ground and smashed. Melody crouched down and fingered the broken ceramic. She lifted out a tiny black sphere. "Bingo."

My pulse kicked up. We had something. "What is it?"

She snorted, her lips curling up in a contemplative smile. "A state of the art camera. The images get encrypted so only the owner can decrypt using a unique code."

"What was he trying to capture in his bedroom?"

She arched a brow.

Ew. "Look, say our assumption is correct, that he was deliberately pointing at that camera and it wasn't just a coincidence that he died in that position. Why?"

"Why?"

"Why would he want us to know about the camera?"

Melody locked gazes with me. "Because he wanted us to know what really happened in this room."

My heart was thudding real fast now. "Because he didn't commit suicide …" The hairs on the nape of my neck stood to attention. "Someone killed him."

Melody swallowed, tugged her phone from her pocket, and dialed. "Get a tech team down here to sweep for x-eyes. Yes. I found one. Uh-huh. Okay. I'll meet you here."

"You think there are more?"

"Undoubtedly. If he was murdered, then he may not have been working alone. The cameras could have been his insurance." She pulled herself off the ground. "Get back to the office and brief Murdoch on what we've found. See if he has any leads on the Yamduth case, and maybe you can speak to Kiran,

Shukra's son. See if there's anything else he can tell us about his father. Anyone Shukra was spending a lot of time with, that kind of thing."

The Yamduth case which Henna and I believed was also linked to Shukra. Dammit, Melody needed to know what was going on, especially now that Shukra could have been murdered. IEPEU needed to be in on this.

I took a deep breath. "There's something I need to tell you."

Melody's expression clouded as I filled her in. "How long have you had this information?"

"A couple of days."

She blew out a breath. "I'm glad you told me. I'll get a team down there now. We'll need to sweep the vault for clues."

"Shukra must be involved in the Yamduth case, and if he was working with someone, it could explain the missing pieces of the puzzle."

Melody scraped back her hair and tied it in an upknot. "Be careful, Hunter. If Shukra's accomplice is out there, the hit could still be active."

My stomach churned. "I know."

I left Melody to wait for the tech team and headed to the office to check in with Murdoch. Half an hour for briefing and three attempts to contact Henna with no joy, and I was off to Shaitan Enterprises for a quick interview with Kiran. The boy was refusing to cooperate. The look in his eyes, pure despair, tore at my heart. My gut told me we'd squeezed all the information out of him that we could. My heart told me to leave him to his grief.

Henna was out, and there was no way I was knocking on Vritra's door. And so there was nothing to do but head home and wait for Melody's call. I was almost out the door when the IEPEU came striding through in their uniforms.

Fanny sat up straighter. She reached for her phone and jabbed a few buttons but didn't pick up the receiver.

Probably a code to alert security that law enforcement was on the premises. A second later, Rajan came striding out of the office, followed closely by another two asura. The officers stopped at the reception desk, and Rajan met them. He shook his head, and the officer in charge held up a touch screen pad. Probably a warrant to search the vault.

Shit. This was what I'd been afraid of, what I'd hoped to avoid by finding answers myself. But the evidence that had come to light today, plus the threat of a djinn invasion, gave me no choice. The least I could do was make this as painless as possible.

I walked over to the reception desk, and Fanny's gaze fell on me. Her lips tightened. She must know I worked for the IEPEU.

"Hey, Rajan." I smiled up at him. "Can you grab Vritra for us please?"

He blinked down at me. "They say they have a search warrant."

"Yeah, they kinda do, and it's important."

His brows snapped down. "You knew about this."

"Yes. And believe me, if it wasn't imperative, we wouldn't be here."

The lifts at the back slid open, and Vritra came storming out. His face was like thunder, his eyes flashing dangerously.

Crappity crap.

I stepped around Rajan to intercept the dragon asura. “Let me explain.”

He speared me with his fiery gaze. “I can take it from here, Miss Hunter. Your assistance is not required.”

It was a clear dismissal, and man, did it hurt. Fanny smirked, and my hand itched to slap the smile off her face.

“Come with me,” Vritra said to the IEPEU operatives. I left them to it and made for the exit. I’d done nothing wrong here. He’d had no right to be so dismissive, or look at me in that accusing way.

Fuck him.

I was out.

22

Melody's call came an hour and a half later, and it wasn't the news I wanted to hear. They'd found five more x-eyes around the house, but decrypting them was going to take some time. Like possibly a day, maybe more. Great. I'd jumped out of the shower and dripped all over the place for nothing.

A knock at the door.

"Hang on a sec!" I grabbed my bathrobe and slipped it on. "Coming."

Banner stood on the doorstep. He glanced down at my robe then up at my face. "You're not ready."

"Ready?"

He made an O with his mouth, and his shoulders slumped. "You forgot."

Forgot? Oh, shit. Pizza and a movie. "Dammit. Banner, I'm so sorry. Look, give me five minutes."

He pouted. "You could just come like that." His eyes twinkled teasingly.

"You wish." I grabbed some clothes and locked myself in the bathroom.

Ten minutes later, we were in his flashy car and parked outside a pizza place. Banner ducked inside to grab our food. My phone beeped with a text from Henna asking if I wanted to grab a drink in Camden. I texted back asking for a rain check, explaining I had plans with Banner tonight.

The door opened, and Banner ducked back into the car. I tucked my phone into my pocket and grabbed the hot pizza box. And then we were away. Five more minutes and we were crunching up Banner's gravel drive.

"This way." Banner led me past the sitting room, all the way to the back of the house and through the patio doors into the garden, painted in the early evening hues of red and orange.

"Where are we going?"

"Cinema room."

"You have a cinema room outside?"

He grinned over his shoulder. "I'm Mal Banner, honey. I have everything."

"Braggy much?"

"In awe much?"

Sure enough, a building came into view between a cluster of carefully planted trees—a low, long, cabin with blacked out windows.

A shiver ran up my spine. "It looks like something out of a slasher movie."

He turned to face me, turning his hands into claws as he walked backward. "Mwahahaha. That's exactly what it is."

"Idiot."

The interior was all recliners with cup holders and movie posters on the walls. And the projector screen was huge.

"Awesome, right?" Banner asked, looking smug. "Take a seat, and I'll grab a selection of movies." He moved over to a storage unit fixed to the wall. "So, how are things with the investigation?"

"Which one?" I drawled. "No. Wait. There *is* only one, because we're pretty sure they're both connected."

"Really?" His voice went up an octave in surprise. "The yamduth case is linked to the asura and djinn kidnappings?"

"Yeah. We found some … stuff at Shukra's today, and we should have solid answers in a few hours."

"Stuff?"

"You know I can't go into details."

"The life of an IEPEU agent. All mystery and danger." He turned to face me. "So, rom com or action?"

"Rom com?" I winced.

He rolled his eyes. "Fine. I have *Maid of honor*?"

"Yeah, that will do."

He popped the movie on and turned on the projector. "Here." He handed me a can of coke. "Phone, please?" He held out his hand.

"What?"

"Cinema rules. No phones."

"I'm expecting a call from Melody."

"And you think they'll have answers in the next hour and a half?"

She'd said a day, maybe more … "Fine." I handed him the mobile, grabbed the can, and took a swig.

Okay. Banner settled down and swung the pizza box round so it was sitting between us. "Let's chill."

An hour and a half later the credits were rolling. I'd forgotten how much I liked the Scottish accent. And how much the particular movie annoyed me. "Seriously, men are so stupid, why wait till she was about to get married to someone else to realize he loved her?"

Banner sat forward. "Because he didn't realize he loved her until she was about to be taken from him."

"You know, I'd love to find a man who was in touch with his feelings and not afraid to share them. Someone who knew what he wanted."

Banner swallowed hard. "Um, prime example sitting right here. Problem is, sometimes, even when we do everything right, even when we are honest, it just isn't enough."

Oh, crap. And there was that look in his eyes. The one he'd hidden from me.

"Mal. I … I don't know what to say."

He smiled sadly. "You don't have to say anything. You are the most amazing woman I've ever met. Even when you have nothing, you make the effort to give. You give your time and energy to the homeless. You give your heart to your friends. You take responsibility when there's every reason to say fuck you. You never needed power to be a hero, Carmella."

My chest grew warm with the heat of his words.

He reached out and tucked a strand of my hair behind my ears. "This has been great. Just the two of us. I wanted it to end on a good note, you know."

My scalp prickled. "End?"

"Being your friend, your confidant has been one of the highlights of my life. I'm going to miss you so much."

Miss me?

A blur in the periphery of my vision was followed by a sharp pain at the side of my head, and then darkness claimed me.

23

Shit, my head ached. I opened my eyes to candlelight and incense. What had happened? I'd been talking to Banner and then … He'd hit me and knocked me out. Adrenaline flooded my veins. I tried to sit up and pain ripped through my arms. Fucking hell. Had he hogtied me?

The room was unfamiliar—a windowless chamber. And where was the door? Something was glowing. I shuffled, trying to swivel my body to see what was casting the strange illumination.

Motherfucker. An orb. A huge orb filled with swirling shifting light. No. Not lights. These were souls. The missing souls we'd been searching for. My cuff … Fuck. I'd taken it off to shower and forgotten to put it back on. My gut twisted, and a sob caught in my throat. Banner was the missing piece of the puzzle.

A door slammed and footsteps echoed off the walls.

“You’re awake.” Banner’s face came into view as he crouched by my head. “Damn. I was hoping you’d sleep through. Just slip away. Looks like drugs don’t work too well on asura.”

“You drugged me?”

He sighed. “Yes. I knocked you out, and then I drugged you. Didn’t want you waking up and going all dragon on me. The cocktail I prepared works as a sedative for you and severs you from your asura power. I didn’t want you to feel any pain. But it looks like a painless death isn’t an option for you.”

Death? He wanted to kill me? “Why are you doing this? I don’t understand. I thought we were friends.”

He smoothed the hair off my brow. “We are. It’s why I know you’ll help me with this. I’ve seen your compassion. How you give of yourself to help others. Now it’s your turn to help me.”

“By dying?”

“It’s the only way, Carmella. If *you* don’t die then *I* will.”

He stood up and walked over to the wall where a long table was set up. “I’ve been dying for a long time—a rare genetic disease that can’t be cured. I accepted it for a while and decided to have fun while I could: women, booze, drugs. I mean, why not, right? And then I found something.” He walked over to me, with a bowl in his hand and crouched by me again. “The Piccadilly High Witch is going senile.” He chuckled. “The old fool kept mistaking me for his predecessor. He told me the original witch’s dirty little secret. They were scientists who discovered the skein and opened a doorway to summon a demon, except … it wasn’t a demon they summoned. It was a cosmic god. This god wanted to taste humanity, experience it through the claiming of souls, and in return, he gave the thirteen scientists access to this skein. There are others out there, you know? Cosmic beings who care nothing for earthly pleasures, but because they experience nothing, they’re unable to self-actualize. It’s a big thing with them apparently.”

He dipped his finger into the bowl and began to smear the wet sticky concoction across my forehead. "Long story short, I got hold of the ritual to summon the cosmic god and made a deal—eternal life for me, in exchange for an orb full of souls for him."

I jerked away from his fingers. "You kidnapped the djinn and ordered the hit on the yaksha?"

"The djinn weren't even from our world. They wouldn't be missed. But we needed someone to retrieve them for us which is where the rakshasa came in, and to control them, we used protsaahan extracted from the apsara. But you know that already, don't you?"

I nodded.

"Yes, so clever. If not for your interference the plan would have gone smoothly. The apsara are so flighty they wouldn't have been missed, and even if they were, we had a cover story ready to download into their memory. We took the protsaahan from them and returned them once we were done. The Kubera tech, Piccadilly coven salvaged from the red zone, was invaluable. But then you interfered, and Shukra and I couldn't use the rakshasa any longer, so we had no choice but to recruit the rogue Yamduth." He sat back on his heels. "We couldn't go after the djinn any longer because they knew what was hunting them." He smiled, and if the situation wasn't so fucked up I'd say he looked impressed. "You really made this difficult."

"But why me? Why did you order a hit on me?"

"Because my time is running out." He glanced at the orb. "It's almost full, and if we'd been allowed to continue using djinn souls, it would have been full weeks ago. Yaksha souls didn't even make a dent, but your soul … the soul of an asura-witch hybrid, now *that* is a powerful thing. It'll fill the orb right up. You're my final kill, Carmella. Your soul will save mine."

My eyes burned. "You'd kill me to save yourself?"

He blew out a breath. "Honestly, when I found out what you were, when I discovered how little time I had left, I wrestled with the decision for hours. But I'm not like you. I don't put others first. I want to live. And if you have to die to make that happen, then so be it."

“How can you be so cold?”

“Impending death can turn the warmest heart to ice.”

“So, all this time you were playing me? Pretending to care about me? Pretending to be my friend while you plotted to have me killed?”

“God, you make it sound so dirty. Look. I do care about you. I think I’m actually a little in love with you. First time a woman has touched my heart this way.” He winked. “I’ve donned a lot of masks in my lifetime. I loved being the guy you turned to for a while. That mask was my favorite. But it won’t save me, so it has to come off.”

The man I’d thought of as my friend, the man I’d felt guilty for not loving, was a killer. How could I have not seen this? How could my gut have been so wrong? Focus. My power was unresponsive, but there had to be a way out of this. Maybe if I kept him talking?

I cleared the lump of terror in my throat. “So, I understand what you were getting out of this, but what about Shukra? How did this benefit him?”

“Shukra got access to the skein.”

“What? How? That’s impossible.”

“I’m sure you saw the symbol on his arm. The infinity sign?” He yanked the collar of his T-shirt down to reveal the same symbol just above his pectoral. “It was a connection to me. And through this connection, he was able to access the skein’s power. I promised him a permanent solution once we were done. Once I was eternal.” He chuckled. “Poor sod didn’t know there is no permanent solution. But he helped me strip you of your connection.” Banner reached for me, lifting the chain around my neck with his index finger. “He helped me forge this chain to mark you for the Daayan. He opened the doorway with an incantation when the witches were chanting at the Mayfair Ball, and he closed it too. But everyone blamed you. The chain made you the key and it was enough for the High Witches to rule in favor of cutting you off.”

“You wanted me weakened so you could kill me.”

“Yes. With your asura and witch power intact you probably would have healed too fast for a killing blow to make a difference. Unfortunately, one of the

Daayan got away and it almost compromised our original deal with the cosmic god. But thanks to you, the Mayfair High Witch has her back, and with a little help from me, after we've mourned your tragic death of course, we'll send the Daayan back." He stood up and walked over to the table again. "The Yamduths' weapons were connected to the orb. A killing blow from those would have yanked your soul straight into the orb over there. But your dragon skin was a problem. Luckily for me, Shukra knew how to pierce dragon skin. He even retrieved the bones for me." He turned to face me. "If I'd known about your cuff and your connection to the djinn, I would have planned for it. But, unfortunately, sometimes you just have to get your hands dirty." He stopped and sighed. "Shukra was a great ally. Shame he made mistakes. He took Urvashi, a apsara not on the list. I never intended her to come to any harm. I like her. But in a way, I should thank him. It forced you into my life, gave me a chance to play hero on a mission to save the apsara. Now that was fun." He held up something slender and white. It gleamed in the candlelight.

"What is that?"

"The last of the dragon bone. Don't worry. I've given it a good sharpen. It'll go in nice and quick, and then it'll be over. I even gave it a little coating of your blood."

Where had he gotten hold of my blood?

He cocked his head. "When you cut your finger, remember?"

My eyes grew hot as anger replaced the chill of betrayal. My dragon stirred and expanded. Whatever he'd given me was wearing off. Thank God. Dragon skin wasn't going to work on this occasion. He had dragon bone. I needed her to take over—to come out and stop him. My vision misted, and I blinked back the tears. Letting her out meant killing Banner … He'd been my friend … He was sick, not just physically but mentally. He needed help. If only there was some other way out of this—some way to get free without hurting him. Power trickled through my limbs as the dragon shook herself awake. The familiar red tinge of her takeover edged my vision. *No other way to be safe.*

"Whoa!" Banner dropped to his knees by me, retrieving something from his pocket.

A syringe.

No.

My dragon roared with fury, and my skin tingled as scales erupted up my legs and across my arms. Yes, now. Please. But then the cold pinch of the needle pierced the unprotected flesh behind my ear. My fingers burned as talons burst from beneath my nails. It was still happening. His drug wasn't working.

"Fuck!" Banner scrambled back.

The dragon roared in triumph, her cry an echo that reverberated into the ether. I bucked, and the ropes holding me prisoner snapped. Rolling onto all fours, I faced him.

"Run, Banner. I won't be in control when she—"

The heat in my limbs began to ebb. What was happening? The power began to dissipate. The drug was doing its thing.

Banner moved closer. "Your concern for my welfare is touching. I'm sorry, Carmella. I really am."

He pushed me onto the ground as the drug began to leaden my limbs. I was going to die. Tears leaked from my eyes, and his face wavered above me as he raised the bone knife high in the air above my heart.

They say your life flashes before your eyes right before you die, but in that moment there was nothing but sheer, unbridled terror.

The splinter and crack of wood had Banner's head whipping up.

"Don't move!"

I knew that voice. Melody. Hope bloomed in my chest.

"Drop the weapon and move away from the woman," Melody said.

I craned my neck as she strode into the chamber, her gun trained on Banner. Her unit spilled in after her, along with someone else.

Henna.

Henna made a move toward me. The edges of my vision darkened as I battled the drug in my system, desperate to stay awake.

"Stay where you are, Miss Ajagar," Melody said.

"Mr. Banner, slowly lower your weapon now."

Banner looked down at me and then back up at the gun-toting woman.

"Trust me," Melody said. "A bullet is much faster than a knife."

His lips curled in a wicked smile. "How about we test that theory?"

The knife came rushing toward me, and then something was crushing me to the ground. A gunshot, a scream, and Henna's eyes staring into mine from her position lying over my chest.

"Henna. What did you do? Henna?"

Her breath was erratic and rapid. "Take care of him … see him … Mother would be proud." She exhaled long and slow and then lay still.

She was dead. Gone. He'd killed her. My rage was like a forest fire, incinerating the drug in my bloodstream, freeing my limbs to sit up and cradle my friend.

Banner lay a few feet to my left, his chest blooming with blood. The shadows covering him receded as the room was filled with light. The orb was glowing brighter and brighter by the second.

"What the fuck is going on?" one of the alpha patrol asked.

Melody grasped me under the armpits and hauled me up. "No. Henna." I wasn't leaving without my friend.

"Drake, grab the dead girl."

I wanted to slap her. This wasn't a dead body it was my friend!

"That thing is gonna blow. We need to get out of here now!" someone else said.

Melody shoved me toward the door and we were off. Drake was right behind us, with Henna slung over his shoulders.

The orb was going to blow. What would happen to the souls? We ran up the tunnel and slammed out of a door right into the cinema room. The earth shook, and the world was filled with intense bright light. We hit the ground, hands over our heads.

And then it was over.

The world was as silent as a tomb.

I sat up to see Henna's body flung on the ground, twisted at an odd angle, her unseeing eyes staring at me almost accusingly.

"Henna …" I crawled over to her, pulled her into my arms, and let the damn burst.

24

They'd found a pile of ashes where Banner's body had been. The orb was nothing but a shell. The souls were gone. Paimon had his answers and our world was safe from invasion, but my friend was dead.

I slugged from the bottle of tequila. Two days. It had been two days, and Vritra refused to answer my calls. Shaitan Enterprises was on lockdown, in mourning, and I hadn't been invited.

This was my fault. If I'd paid attention, I may have picked up on the clues. If I hadn't been so quick to trust Banner and condemn everyone else, this could have been avoided. I couldn't face anyone. Not Honey, not Urvashi, and not Victor. And Vritra …

What the fuck was I going to say to him even if I did manage to get an audience?

The tech team had decrypted the x-eyes and seen Banner kill Shukra. He'd wanted us to believe we had our man. To lull us into a false sense of security and buy time to finish his plan, and he'd almost succeeded. When Melody had been unsuccessful getting hold of me she'd called around and managed to get a hold of Henna who'd told her I was with Banner, and the rest … well, it was history, or at least it should be, except whatever had happened in that underground chamber … my gut told me it wasn't over. But tonight was for drinking tequila and raising shot glass after shot glass to the woman who'd saved my life.

Someone hammered on the door.

"Fuck off!" I took another slug

The door flew open, and Mira strode in, pig tails bobbing. She kicked the door shut and flung herself on the sofa beside me before making a grab for the bottle.

I yanked it out of her reach. "Piss off and get your own."

She glared at me, her eyes glistening with moisture.

What the fuck? Was she about to bawl?

"Here." I handed her the bottle. "No need to get so emotional."

She put it to her lips, tipped back her head, and glugged it down, all the way down to the last drop.

"Dammit, Mira! I needed that."

She wiped her mouth. "Yeah, so did I."

"What happened to you?"

"Paimon just fired me."

"What?"

Mira's bottom lip wobbled. "I've been his s-s—"

"Sidekick?"

She threw a lethal look my way. "Sentinel forever. He was my lord. And now, because of *her*, he's set me aside."

Her? "Alara?"

"Yes, Alara. That bitch makes demands, and he scrambles about to make them happen. Apparently, I make her feel *uncomfortable*."

I stared at her unblinkingly.

"What? It's my job to have Paimon's back, not to make his bitches feel comfortable." She crossed her arms over her chest.

"So, what now? You get another position as a sentinel elsewhere?"

She swallowed. "That's not how it works. Once you've been claimed by a lord you're useless to another." She sniffed. "I'm useless and fucking homeless."

He'd abandoned her for his betrothed, a woman he was marrying for political reason. He'd thrown out a loyal sentinel for Alara? Indignation on her behalf, resentment toward Alara, and anger at Paimon mingled in my chest.

"Fuck him. Fuck her. And fuck that. You can stay with me until we get you sorted."

She turned to look at me, her eyes widening? "You mean it?"

"Damn straight, I mean it."

"Maybe I can be your sentinel, unofficially of course?"

"Whoa. Hold up. I don't need a sentinel, but maybe … maybe we can be friends."

She blinked rapidly as if processing the proposition and examining the concept. “Friends.”

“Yes. You know. We hang out. Go out together. Share stories, secrets, that kind of thing?”

He face lit up in comprehension. “And if someone threatens you, I kill them.”

I dropped my head into my hands. Okay, maybe this was a discussion best handled when sober. I grabbed a twenty from my purse. “Why don’t you go grab us a bite to eat and then we can have a proper gossip.”

She bounced up.

“Oh, and if you’re going to be staying with me for a while, you might want to look a little older?”

She grinned, that wicked gleam back in her eyes. Her body blurred and morphed until she was standing before me in the body of a hot, twenty-something dude.

“Better?” she said in her new deep masculine voice.

“And preferably female.”

“Spoilsport.” She shifted again, this time into her Caro form. “See you in a few.”

I flopped back onto the bed. So much for taking a time out. Henna's face flashed before my eyes. Her final words. Her final wish. I owed her my life. I owed her everything.

The phone rang and I answered.

"Carmella, dear."

"Aunt. Where are you? It's been over a week."

"I found your mother."

"You did. And, what did she say?"

"Honey. I'll be with you in a couple of days, and I'll tell you everything then."

"Seriously? You're going to make me wait?"

"Oh, dear. I shouldn't have phoned. Silly mistake."

"Aunt!"

"It's really not news to be delivered over the phone."

"How about I be the judge of that?"

She took a shuddering breath. "Honey. Your mother … well, she's not your biological mother."

Her words rang in my ears.

"Carmella, are you there? Are you listening to me?"

Where was the shock and horror? Had I somehow always known? Sensed it, maybe? "Yes. Yes, I'm here. Does she know who my real mother is?"

"No, dear. Do you remember when you went for blood tests when you were thirteen? You'd been having dizzy spells and your mother was concerned."

"I remember."

"Well, the blood tests proved that you couldn't be hers."

"Is that why she just stopped loving me?"

"Oh, honey. I really should be there with you."

"No. Tell me what she said. I need to know."

"She told me she went to the Mayfair Mansion where she'd given birth. She demanded to speak to the High Witch, and she got her answers."

"And?"

"That's it. She couldn't tell me anymore."

"What do you mean she couldn't tell you anything more?"

"I mean she physically could not speak the words."

"A witch's oath."

"Yes. Carmella. You need to be wary. The Mayfair High Witch cannot be trusted. We don't know if she played a hand in this, or how much of a part she played. She could be dangerous."

"She could be the one that bound my powers in the first place."

"Listen to me, dear. Let it go. You're alive and you're safe and you have a life. So they cut you off from the skein, so what? You don't need it. Don't be defined by power, sweetheart. Just live your life as you."

"Thank you."

We said our goodbyes.

She was right. I didn't have to be defined by the power that coursed through my veins. The power should be defined by who I already was, and yeah, I was totally cool with that. But I wasn't cool with letting this slide. I wasn't cool with not knowing where I truly came from or why I hadn't been allowed to be raised by my biological mother, or why my powers had been bound. Banner had revealed that it wasn't me that had opened the doorway to release the Daayan, so that couldn't be why my power had been bound as a child. The only explanation was that someone had been trying to hide me. But the question was from who, and why?

There was only one person who might have the answer to all these questions.

The High Witch.

Friend or foe, it wasn't clear, so I wasn't going to go in guns blazing. No. It was time to play the long game.

The door slammed open, and Mira strode in with a bag of food and a bottle of tequila.

Playing the long game would require stamina. Stamina and a clear head. Taking the tequila off her, I stood and padded over to the kitchen.

"What are you doing?" Mira asked.

I unscrewed the lid and poured the whole thing down the sink. "Pulling my shit together, that's what."

I was asura, whether they liked it or not, and one of ours was dead. My friend was fucking dead. There was no hiding from that fact. No running away. Henna had asked me for something, and I was going to deliver, even if I had to smash down their bloody doors to get inside.

WHAT THE HECK was I thinking? There was no smashing down these doors, not without turning full dragon. I contemplated it for a millisecond and discarded the idea. Wait, the buzzer—which had been dead the day before—was lit up. Did that mean someone was monitoring it? Pulse racing, I hit call. The intercom buzzed, and buzzed, then buzzed some more.

Come on! There had to be someone about.

"Hello?" a male voice answered. Possibly Rajan?

"It's Carmella Hunter. I need to come in."

"About fucking time."

The doors buzzed followed by a soft click. They were open, and I was through.

Rajan met me in the foyer, his expression stormy. "You should have come sooner."

"What? I did come. The doors were locked and the intercom thingy was dead. I called too, hundreds of times."

"You could have used your access card to get in at any time," he said.

I placed my hands on my hips. "I don't have a damned access card. I gave it back, remember?"

"Oh." His shoulders slumped. "That explains it. The asura have being going nuts. One half pissed at you for going AWOL, the other making excuses."

"What about Vritra?" It was him I cared about the most. Had I just thought that?

Rajan blew out his cheeks and shook his head. "That's the problem. Vritra has gone full dragon. We managed to get him locked up in the vault, but we can't risk going in after him. It's been two days. If he doesn't shift back soon, we may lose him to the dragon completely."

"What does that mean?"

"It means he may not be able to change back into his human form."

"He knows this though, right? So why would he stay in dragon form, why … Oh …" He was running from his grief.

"He doesn't have to face what's happened in his dragon form," Rajan confirmed. "In that form, he can avoid the pain."

"Well, someone needs to go down there and remind him. Someone needs to wake him up."

Rajan smiled wryly. "Yeah, I was hoping you'd say that."

"Me?" My voice was a squeak.

He grimaced. "You're the only other asura who can shift. If he attacks, you can defend yourself."

Great. "But I won't be in control. I have no idea what will happen."

"If we do nothing, we'll lose him."

No. We couldn't lose him. I'd do this, for Henna, for the asura, and for Vritra. "Take me to him."

———

THE CHAMBER WAS shrouded in darkness and the scent of jasmine lingered in the air. My stomach tightened in anxiety, but there was no going back now. I was here—walking into the dragon's underground lair, knowing full well that he might rip me to shreds. I was the reason his daughter was dead. She'd given her life to save me. My stupid blindly trusting nature had killed his only offspring. I owed him this.

The gloom edged into amber light, and a huge stone table came into view. The skeleton of a huge beast lay sprawled across the stone, the bone a buttery yellow in the amber light. Where was Vritra?

I felt his presence at my back before my dragon did, and then she was awake and vibrating with wariness. My body tensed, ready to flee, and every hair on my body stood to attention. The presence at my back wasn't the Vritra I knew. It was wild and primal. It was the dragon.

His dragon heat enveloped me, and hot breath blew across the top of my head.

"Vritra, I need to speak to you." My voice trembled and I cleared my throat. "I can't do that if you're in dragon form."

Shadows closed in and a gust of air threw my hair into my face as he rushed past—huge and fast and lethal.

"Vritra, please."

Where was he? My dragon tentatively reached out with her power. Even she sensed the danger—the knife's edge that Vritra walked.

The lights flickered and dimmed.

"Vritra?"

The shadows to my left shifted, and I turned my head to see two huge ember eyes watching me from the darkness. My stomach tightened in fear. He was huge, bigger than I'd imagined. He moved toward me, his head—a meter off the ground—was a ridged expanse of ebony scales. Obsidian … He was an obsidian dragon, and my heart lurched in yearning and awe, even as my knees quivered in fear. My fingers itched to reach out and touch him.

He wasn't attacking. Not yet. Did he know who I was? Rajan had warned me he was out of his mind, and he may not recognize me, but he was watching me almost speculatively. He'd been in dragon form for over two days. He needed to shift back before he got stuck this way.

Mouth dry and heart slamming against my ribs, I took a tentative step toward him. He huffed, and hot air billowed out of his nostrils, searing my skin. I reached out and slowly, oh so fucking slowly, placed my hand on the space between those immense nostrils. Okay, I was doing this. Touching him, and he wasn't attacking. The scales were dry and smooth. The urge to caress them swept through me, forcing me to clench my free hand to quash the impulse.

"Vritra. Please. Come back to us. We need you."

He blinked, slow and lazy.

Another step and I was practically feeding myself to him. He'd lost two people he loved in the space of a couple of days. This powerful dynamic man, who everyone relied on to be their anchor, was now adrift—slave to his grief and the beast within. He was shutting out the pain the only way he knew how. By manipulating him to shift back, I would be forcing him to confront the loss. I'd be offering him pain. But without it, there was no moving forward.

I laid my other hand on his huge snout. "I loved her too. I loved Henna. She died to save me, Vritra. She died so I could live. You hear me?"

His eyes flared, the ember catching the light in a way that made them look like flames burned within. My body shuddered. What was I doing? Pissing off a dragon? But then maybe this was the only way to bring him back. I needed to make him feel something, to force him to turn on his humanity and confront me.

"I'm here and she isn't. How does that make you feel, Vritra? Huh? Come on. Tell me." He jerked away from me, knocking me on my arse and then rising above me, his huge serpentine body holding his massive head aloft as he gazed down on me with disdain.

"Come on, Vritra. Your daughter is dead and you're hiding down here while her body rots upstairs. Don't you think she deserves more? Don't you think she deserves better?"

A roar filled the chamber, battering my eardrums and rattling my bones. My dragon surged upward covering me in armor just as his tail swished round to slam into me. I was airborne for the longest moment and then hit the ground, skidding backward, scales scraping rock.

Vritra advanced, fury lighting up his eyes. Oh, boy. I'd successfully rattled the beast, and he was spoiling for a fight. And if it was a fight he wanted then … I let go of the reins and allowed my dragon to take over. The world bled into crimson and grew smaller, and then a freight train slammed into me, and darkness took over.

Flashes, images, talons, fangs, heat, and scales clashing, I was inside her head but locked up tight, safe from the trauma. What was happening? How was I doing? A flash of pain, a crushing weight, and then the darkness receded. The world was crimson for a moment but amber light took over.

I was back … On the ground and … naked? A breath caressed the back of my neck.

"Carmella … I'm sorry. So sorry."

Vritra. He was holding me, my back to his front. It was over. I turned in his arms, wincing as pain lanced up my side.

"Hey, it's okay. You're back." I caressed his stubbled jaw, looking down on him. "It's all right."

He stared up at me, pain etched into his face. “No. It’s not all right. She’s gone. My little girl is gone.”

My eyes burned with emotion. Vritra reached up to trace the tracks of tears on my cheeks.

“She left me.” His voice was a trembling whisper.

Something inside me cracked and melted. I pulled him closer, cushioning his head against my bare breasts. “I’m here. And I’m not going anywhere.”

And then the asura dragon broke down, and I held him while he sobbed. Henna was gone. She’d given her life to save mine. She’d believed in me enough to sacrifice herself. I owed her this. I owed her my life. Her sacrifice would not be in vain.

Banner had manipulated events to take my magick. It was time to claim it back, to become whole. To become the person I was meant to be, and if someone came after me, then they’d have a fucking magick wielding dragon to deal with.

To be continued…

Check out the excerpt for Embracing Magick, book 3 in The Witch Blood Chronicles and then click the image to order your copy.

1

"I wasn't expecting a welcoming committee," Melody said as we drew up to the terraced family home in Camden.

People lined the sidewalk, some dressed for work, others still in their pajamas and slippers. A woman held a squirming baby on her hip, jiggling him every time he fussed. And a group of teenagers hovered on the pavement across the street.

A smartly dressed, elderly couple exited the house and walked toward us just as the IEPEU vans zoomed around the corner and onto the tidy residential street. Citizens stumbled back as the sleek vehicles came to a halt, and operatives jumped out. Tech equipment was unloaded, and Melody and I exited her corvette to meet the couple who'd called this in.

Mr. and Mrs. Finch were the parents of Mr. Stanley Finch, who until last night had been a resident at this address.

"Where are they? Where's my family?" the woman demanded. If not for the tears in her eyes, I would have taken offense at her tone, but considering the circumstances, the poor woman had every reason to be upset.

"I assure you we will do everything we can to find out, Mrs. Finch." My tone was deliberately confident and soothing.

The man snorted. "Like you did the last time, and the time before? How many families have to go missing before you people do something?"

A murmur rose up from the gathered neighbors.

"They were here last night," the woman with the baby called out. "I saw Stan putting the bin out."

"What's going on?" someone else cried.

"It could be us next. The fucking government don't give a toss."

Great, the last thing we needed was an angry mob. I stepped off the curb and into the road. “Please!” I held up my hands. “Everybody, go back into your homes and get on with your day. In order to solve this case, we’re going to need your co-operation. An operative will be doing the rounds to speak to you all shortly. Please provide the operative with any relevant information. If you don’t have the time right now, then we’ll make an appointment to speak with you. But please, allow us to do our job. The longer we wait, the colder the trail gets.”

Stanley’s mother whimpered, and her husband put his arm around her, pulling her close.

“Just do what you have to do,” he said. “Find my son, my daughter-in-law and my grandbabies.”

“Yes, sir.”

Leaving the couple outside we headed into the house, knowing exactly what we would find but dreading it all the same.

***

The bare room stared back at me. Barren and clean, not even a mini dust bunny to say it had ever been lived in. The whole house was the same—picked clean. If not for the fact that the family had been here yesterday, there'd be no case. But this was the tenth vanishing in the city. Ten families gone—poof, overnight. Their relatives, friends, neighbors none the wiser. How? How could you move out all your shit in one night *and* clean the house *and* have no one notice? You couldn't, that's how? Guaranteed there'd be no trace of removal van hire, and the cars they'd owned were parked outside on the street—also picked clean. All this, coupled with the fact that Stanley's parents had travelled down from up north to spend the week with them, suggested that this family hadn't disappeared of their own volition.

There was some strange shit going on, and it was my responsibility to find out just what.

"Anything?" Melody strode in, scanning the room. "This is getting ridiculous.

"You've done a sweep downstairs?"

She nodded.

"Up here is clear." I walked out into the hallway. "No basement. Attic? Did you check?"

"Harriet did. It's empty."

She headed for the stairs, but my feet remained rooted to the spot as my asura power expanded in warning. "Wait. We're missing something."

I exhaled and relinquished control to the power within. A few months ago, my heart would have fluttered in panic at handing over the reins to the dragon inside. But over the course of the last six weeks, we'd come to an understanding—I let her out to play now and then, and she respected my boundaries. My feet carried me to the hatch in the ceiling.

"You want to check again?" Melody asked.

"Yeah."

I yanked the rope to bring down the steps. The dragon sensed something up there, and it was rarely, if ever, wrong. Training with Vritra for the last six weeks, sparring with Gita and Kiran and the other asura—who hadn't gone easy on me despite getting their arses handed to them by my dragon—had honed my skills. I made sure to leave the skein untapped in those matches. Hardly fair to double up on my opponent, besides it was the asura power I needed to master, the skein came naturally, and man, did it feel good to have it back. Once the coven discovered Banner's deception, and checked out the enchanted chain he'd given me, there'd been no choice for them but to give me back my connection to the skein. Which opened up the question of who the heck had bound my powers and why? If it wasn't to prevent me from doing dodgy things with the skein, then what was it?

At the top of the steps was a light switch. I flicked it on, but nothing happened. "Melody? You got a flashlight?"

She handed me her penlight. It would have to do. Climbing up into the attic, nothing more than a crammed crawl space, I swept the light over the boxes and bags of old toys and Christmas decorations. Not so clean up here. What was I missing? Fuck. There had to be something. The dragon was never wrong.

"Anything?" Melody asked.

Shimmying up into the crawl space, light between my teeth, I began moving the boxes and bags. A soft whimper caught my attention, closely followed by a strangled sob. My hand came into contact with something smooth and crackly, and then the mound moved.

I yanked my hand away. "What the fuck!"

"Carmella?" Melody called up the stairs.

It was a silver blanket. Like one of those insulation ones you used when backpacking, and something—no, someone—was underneath it.

Keeping my voice low and calm, I reached for the edge of the blanket. "It's all right. I'm not going to hurt you."

"Please...you can't take it off. If you take it off, they'll find me."

"I'm with the IEPEU. I promise you're safe now."

The body under the blanket quivered. "They took them. They took them all, and it's my fault. All my fault."

"Who took them?"

Another sob. "The aliens."

Oh, lord. "I'm going to take the blanket off now and we can talk about this over a nice hot drink, okay."

"No!"

I tugged the blanket off the body, and for a moment there he was, a pimply teenage boy with overly gelled hair and a heavy metal T-shirt, and then … he was gone.

Other books by Debbie Cassidy

The Gatekeeper Chronicles

Coauthored with Jasmine Walt

Marked by Sin

Hunted by Sin

Claimed by Sin

The Witch Blood Chronicles

(*Spin off to the Gatekeeper Chronicles*)

Binding Magick

Defying Magic

Embracing Magick

The Fearless Destiny Series

Beyond Everlight

Into Evernight

The Sleeping Gods Series

Forest of Demons

Desert of Destiny

Novellas

Blood Blade

Books under the pen name Amos Cassidy

The Shadowlands Series

Shadow Reaper

Shadow Eater

Shadow Destiny

The Crimson Series

Crimson Midnight

Crimson Darkness

Crimson Dawn

Crimson Chaos

Standalones

Aurora

Hawthorn

Novellas

Raven's Call

Scarlett's Path

A Kiss of Silver

Tainted Snow

Ash Rising